I0698788

DIANE E. TATUM

Mysteries at Kate's Bed & Breakfast, Book 4:

Christmas Wedding Disruptions

Kate's
Bed & Breakfast

415 Spring Street
Adams, TN 37010
kate@katesb&b.com

By Diane E. Tatum

To Christ, my Rock and Salvation.

To my family.
My love, Ken, for 46 years and counting.
My sons, Dan and Brad who have sought God's will and are working in the fields they felt God wanted them to pursue.
My daughters-in-law, Becca and Julie who are my daughters in all ways.
My grandsons, Ethan, Kellan, Paul, and Jonathan, whom I love with all my heart and desire all the best for their lives.

DIANE E. TATUM

*And Elisha prayed, "Open his eyes, L*ORD*, so that he may see." Then the L*ORD *opened the servant's eyes, and he looked and saw the hills full of horses and chariots of fire all around Elisha.   2 Kings 6:17 NIV*

*And surely **I am with you always**, to the very end of the age. Matthew 28:20b NIV*
Then Peter came to Jesus and asked, "Lord, how many times shall I forgive my brother or sister who sins against me? Up to seven times?" Jesus answered, "I tell you, not seven times, but seventy-seven times." Matthew 18:21-22 NIV

In the same way, the Spirit helps us in our weakness. We do not know what we ought to pray for, but the Spirit himself intercedes for us through wordless groans. And he who searches our hearts knows the mind of the Spirit, because the Spirit intercedes for God's people in accordance with the will of God. And we know that in all things God works for the good of those who love him, who have been called according to his purpose. Romans 8:26-28 NIV

We are never alone, friends. Though the mysteries, disasters, catastrophes, and profound mistakes enter our lives, God knows our struggle and will work on our behalf. And when we don't even know how to pray, the Holy Spirit interprets our prayers to Father God through Jesus Christ.

Chapter 1

Preparing for Christmas …

Kate placed her mother's nativity set on the mantel above the living room fireplace. The handcrafted German nativity set included the family, a shepherd, and several animals. One of the oxen's horns was chipped. She placed the animals on the mantel first. then the people. Last of all, she set Jesus in the manger front and center. As her mom had placed each piece, she would read a scripture about it. The list of scriptures was not in the box. Kate had found her mom's Bible in the same box with the nativity set. Could the list be in Mom's old Bible?

It was a wonder Kate had found the old nativity scene at all. She'd not seen it since her mom's death from cancer. Her father was not 'religious' even though Mom was, in his words, 'hyper-religious.' He no doubt packed it away all those years ago, like he packed away all Kate's relationships in Adams, TN. He didn't like her hanging out with Aunt Katharine during the summers. That meant her relationship with Will, Billy then, was packed away as well.

After her dad severed her ties to Adams, he died in a car accident, leaving her to do college and start her professional career in the music business alone. Aunt Katharine's dementia and eventual death had brought Kate back to the only place she'd felt at home.

I guess he'd be appalled that I'm living here in Aunt Katharine's house and marrying 'that boy.' She laughed. *Guess I'm becoming religious too.*

The security alarm chimed as the front door opened and closed.

"Katie! It's Maddy!" It was Will's mom who called out to her.

"In the living room, Mom." It still felt odd to call her 'Mom,' but she was the only mom she had now. She'd been Kate's mom's best friend and oozed love in everything she did.

Maddy waltzed into the living room carrying her large tote bag of a purse and a larger box. "Happy Thursday! I found Christmas ornament kits at Michaels in Clarksville. I couldn't remember how many people you had this weekend, so I bought all they had." She dropped her purse and carried the box to the dining table. "Aren't these just the cutest things?"

Kate peeked into the box, and all she saw were sequins, lots and lots of sequins. "What am I looking at?"

"I know; it's stunning. Merry-go-round horses, apples, stars, and poinsettias covered in sparkly sequins." Maddy was over-the-moon excited.

"Are we talking about glue or straight pins?" Kate pictured sequins all over the floor and clogging the vacuum cleaner.

"Not sure. I'll come and help with this crafty stuff. Don't you worry about it." Maddy took the box into the kitchen. "It'll be great!"

Thank goodness Kate's plans were not as ambitious as her Thanksgiving dinners every weekend in November had been. The five-day weekend with the murder mystery 'game' had been beyond disastrous. Not as many guests had signed on for each weekend in December, either. This first weekend's activities included decorating the house and tree, making and decorating Christmas cookies, and making Maddy's Christmas ornaments.

Two families with two grade-school-aged children planned to arrive on Friday around three o'clock. Kate planned a beef stew and cornbread dinner on Friday. Easy, hearty, and welcoming.

While Katie prepared for the weekend, Will wandered the backwoods with his dad, hunting for mistletoe to shoot out of trees. He was determined to fill the house with it for their wedding on the twenty-third. He'd also promised to bring back a tree for their first December weekend guests to help decorate.

"Does that look like mistletoe?" Dad pointed out a ball of greenery high in a tree.

"Maybe, I'm really not sure." Will wasn't a hunter or a forestry major. Engineering was his thing. That and

Katie Winslow. On the twenty-third, God willing, she'd be Katie Bell. It's all he could think about. Three more weeks.

"Son, are you with me?" Dad tapped on his shoulder.

"Yes, sir. There's a lot going on this month." Will felt the blood rushing into his face. "I'm thinking about Katie and the wedding. Sorry."

His dad laughed. "Son, if you weren't thinking about Katie, I'd be worried. Marriage is serious business. Katie is a wonderful girl. It will be fine." He aimed and fired his shotgun into the tree, bringing down the ball of green. "Yep, mistletoe. How much of this stuff do you want?"

"As much as we can find, Dad."

By the time they'd finished tromping around in the woods, the pickup bed was full of mistletoe and a decent-sized Christmas tree. Will's fingers were tingly from the cold, and his face felt frozen. *Unusual for this time of year in Tennessee.*

"Son? You're lost again." His dad's voice brought him back to consciousness.

"Sorry. I was just thinking it was cold for this time of year. Like a January cold." Will rubbed his hands together. "What do I do with the mistletoe to hang it in the house?"

"That's a question to ask your mom. I just do the shooting." His dad laughed. "I'd say you have a day's worth of wrapping ribbon around bunches of the stuff."

I'm an idiot. I don't need to spend a day preparing the stuff and then another day hanging it. And I've got the tree to get in the house.

"Billy Bell! Your head is in the clouds today." His dad pulled up in front of Katie's house. "Where do you want to put all of this mistletoe?"

"Let's put it in the cellar. It will stay cool down there. The tree goes in the foyer beside the steps. There's a stand already waiting."

Dad climbed out of the driver's seat and let down the tailgate. Will grabbed the tree first and his dad took hold on the other side, then they hauled it up onto the porch.

Katie was waiting for them. "It's beautiful!" She wrapped her arms around him and whispered, "I'm glad you didn't get lost in the woods. You were gone a long time."

Will kissed her. "Never! There's too much to do to get lost somewhere."

His dad burst into belly laughs. "Katie, he's been lost in his mind all morning, probably thinking about you and that wedding."

"We have so much to do before the wedding, including our weekend guests coming tomorrow and decorations to get down from the attic." Katie kissed him back. "Did you find any mistletoe?"

Maddy joined them on the front porch. "Looks like the pickup bed is full of it. What are you going to do with so much mistletoe, Billy?"

He grinned. "Hang it up all over the house. Any excuse to kiss my bride-to-be."

"Do you need an excuse to kiss me?" Katie's eyes sparkled in the sunlight.

"Never, but let's go inside before my face freezes." Will hugged Katie, then followed her into the house.

As he stepped into the house, his phone began

ringing. Not a number he recognized. "Hello. This is Will Bell."

"Will Bell, this is Anthony Clarence. Remember me from your short former employment in Nashville?"

What does he want? "Of course, what can I do for you?"

Anthony cleared his throat. "Any chance you're ready to abandon your small business?"

"No. I don't have a lot of work, but I do have some. My fiancée and I are running a bed and breakfast as well." *And making no money from it.* Will shook his head.

Anthony continued. "I have a job for you. You can rejoin the firm, or I can contract it out to you. Are you interested?"

"Can you send me the information on it, so I can make an informed decision?"

"Sure. I still have your email. I'll send information about it to you. But you can't share it with anyone, especially your girl. This project is off the books, so to speak."

Will concluded the conversation and stared at the phone in his hand. *What is this all about?*

Chapter 2

Preparing for weekend #1 …

Early on Friday, Kate greeted Sarah at the front door early. She carried trays of pastries and bread from her bakery for the first weekend of December's guests.

"So glad to see you this morning. Those apple turnovers smell amazing! My guests will love them. Do you have time to come in?" Kate swung open the front door.

Sarah carried the tray into the kitchen. "Absolutely! Maybe fifteen minutes."

Kate grinned. "I want to show you something."

They settled the bread in the kitchen and took the tray back to the front door. Then Kate led Sarah up the stairs.

She invited Sarah into her bedroom to see Aunt Katharine's wedding dress. The hanger hung on a wall hook, displayed with the pearl necklace her father bought on her sixteenth birthday. On the floor below it rested the off-white shoes she'd bought to match the old lace of the dress.

"Oh, Kate! This dress is amazing. How did you

remove the smoke from the attic fire and the age from the lace?" Sarah fingered the old fabric.

"I took it to a dry cleaner who hooked me up with a specialty cleaner. He dipped it in magic sauce." Kate laughed. "I have no idea what they used, but it worked."

"Magic sauce?" Sarah laughed too. "I'm surprised you could find shoes to match since it's not really cream but not really white either."

"The magic of Amazon. I ordered about ten pairs of shoes and then sent back the ones that wouldn't work. I did that about five times before feeling satisfied with a pair that matched and were comfortable enough to walk down that staircase."

Sarah covered her mouth and laughed. "Not sure, but that sounds like Amazon abuse."

"Hey! As long as they offer 'Try Before You Buy,' I'm within their shopping guidelines. I feel bad for the UPS guy." Kate giggled. It was nice to have a girlfriend to share all this with.

"What about a veil?" Sarah looked at the pearls.

"I don't have one." Kate sighed. "The attic fire destroyed the original veil. Finding shoes to match was so hard. It's just one more thing to deal with. It's not important enough to me to stress over it. After all, I could go barefoot, but in December it will be too cold to walk outside that way. Shoes are important. And I spent a fortune cleaning the dress."

"I understand." Sarah fingered the pearl necklace. "Why are you getting married here instead of at the church? You wouldn't have to worry about stairs there."

"This was my Great Aunt Katharine's house as well as my grandmother's and great-grandmother's. I spent every summer here until my mom got cancer when I was eleven. Having the ceremony and reception here feels like having Mom and Aunt Katharine at my wedding."

"So, will your dad walk you down the stairs?" Sarah plopped onto Kate's bed.

"No, he's gone, in a car accident, when I was eighteen. Those pearls were one of the last gifts he gave me." Kate slumped down beside Sarah. "I'm really all alone except for Will and his family."

"And me. Let me be your best friend." Sarah took her hand. "I'd better get the rest of my deliveries finished, so my sister Jane isn't left alone for too long at the bakery. She works really hard, but she's not able to make decisions alone. Thanks for showing me your wedding finery."

Kate was sad to see Sarah leave so soon, but they both had work to do today.

After seeing her off, Kate went through the house, making sure all was ready for her new guests. She started the beef stew in the Crock-Pot. Before long, the house filled with the tantalizing aroma of beef and onions.

The kitchen door slammed.

"It smells good in here." Will grabbed Kate around the waist and snuggled into her neck with kisses. "Is that beef stew for tonight?"

Kate giggled. "Your fashionable stubble tickles."

"And you love it." He kissed her shoulder.

"I do." Kate hugged him.

"I thought we were running a bed-and-breakfast. Why are you fixing dinner for our guests?" He leaned against the counter, pulling Kate along with him.

Kate shrugged. "It seems like the welcoming thing to do, especially in a small town with few options for eating out."

"Springfield's not that far away. They could drive twelve miles and get almost anything they wanted. Fixing dinner as well is unnecessary." Will gave her a concerned look. "You'll burn out trying to be all for everyone who darkens our door."

"I can't change it now. I already offered stew and cornbread for tonight." Kate knew he was right. "But what we serve here is hospitality." She pointed out the cross-stitch Maddy had made. "Entertaining angels unaware."

"Hospitality is one thing. This is supposed to be a business, after all. Overdoing costs money and dings our bottom line. We're not making any money so far." Will kissed her nose. "I love you, Katie. You are changing my life every day."

"What have you been doing all morning?" Kate sniffed. "You smell green."

"I've been in the cellar creating bundles of mistletoe. Mom came and helped me." He held up his green hands. "I should probably scrub up before lunch."

Kate took his hand and examined it. "You also have nicks and scratches. Are you sure this is worth the trouble.?"

"Yes, ma'am. I want all the excuses I can have to kiss you, Katie." He took her into his warm embrace and kissed her with growing intensity.

Kate closed her eyes and enjoyed the closeness of her man, his masculine cologne, and his mistletoe green smell. She had a lifetime to enjoy him. God had given her an amazing gift.

"Mm! You smell so good." Will snuggled again into her shoulder.

"You're probably smelling beef stew." Kate hugged him closer.

"You're probably right. What's for lunch?"

Kate burst into giggles. "Are you kidding me? You turn a romantic interlude into a request for food?"

He squeezed tighter. "You know what they say. The way to a man's heart is through his stomach."

"From now on I should wear *Eau de Boeuf* perfume?" Kate whispered into his ear.

"No. I don't want any other man smelling you this close." He relaxed in her arms.

"Uh, hum!"

At the sound of the voice, Kate and Will jumped apart.

Will's brother Joe stood in the kitchen doorway with his arms crossed. "Hope I'm not interrupting anything. The wedding is still three weeks away, you guys."

Will growled. "How long have you been standing there?"

"Long enough!" Joe chuckled.

Will took a swipe at him. Joe repelled his 'brotherly attack.'

"How are Sally and Baby Mandy doing?" Kate gave Joe a brief hug. "Is there something I can do for you?"

"They're both fine. Sally wants to invite you both for dinner. I told her you had guests coming in and wouldn't want to leave them alone in the house." Joe perched on a kitchen stool.

Kate had never noticed just how much Joe and

Will resembled each other. Same dark brown hair, same stubble, same dark brown eyes. But Joe was a good three inches taller than Will, and farming had left Joe more muscular than his college-educated engineer brother.

Will spoke up. "You're right. Andy and the sheriff are ready to shut us down for being a nuisance. If something happened and we weren't on the premises, well, our business would be done."

"Is there a better time I can suggest to Sally?" Joe took a cookie from the jar on the counter.

"Tuesday or Wednesday night should be safe." Kate raised her eyebrows and looked at Will.

"Sure. Tuesday or Wednesday if nothing weird happens." Will snagged a cookie too.

"I'll tell her. Hope everything goes the way it should this weekend. You're due for some blessings instead of curses." He hugged Kate then pulled Will into a bro hug.

Kate and Will followed him to the porch. "Thanks for the invitation. I'd love to eat someone else's food for a change."

After Joe drove away in his truck, Will pulled Kate to him. "Look!" He pointed to the ceiling of the porch. An impressive bunch of mistletoe hung above them gathered with white and red ribbon. Will held her close and kissed her. "I have a lot more where that came from."

Kate kissed him back. "I like it, for many reasons. Merry Christmas, Sweetheart."

"Merry Wedding, my love. Now about lunch…"

After lunch, Will returned to the garage.

He booted up his laptop and rifled through the papers on his desk for the two other jobs for which he had contracts.

I wonder if Anthony's mysterious message has come in. Will scanned his email. Sure enough, one from Anthony. Oddly, it wasn't through his company email. It was Anthony's private address. He opened it.

"Hey, Will!

"Don't open the attachment if you don't want the job. It's a private job brought to me, not to the company. You know how the company is, though. If I take on a contract without declaring it to the higher-ups, I could lose my job. Privacy is the word on this contract. No one can know about it, *capiche*?

"Once you've seen it, you agree to do it. I know that's weird, but it's that kind of job. The pay is $25,000 for the design and installation. Reply to this email, not my work one.

"Anthony"

Will scratched his head. He had to decide whether to take on a secret project, sight unseen? *What kind of deal is this?* Theme music from *The Godfather* filtered through his head. $25,000 for the design and installation? How much would it cost him personally? No one gave away $25,000 for nothing.

On another corner of his desk sat the statements for the B&B for the first two months. In January, Katie and he would be married and had agreed to look at the business to decide if it was profitable. Will hadn't told Katie just how much their business cost them during those two months. He doubted December would be any better. Katie wanted to provide their guests with everything she could. The trick was they couldn't afford to do that at the prices they were charging.

Will's engineering business would need to provide for them, one way or the other. He hesitated. His cursor hovered over the attachment.

Finally, he clicked on it.

Chapter 3

Decorating, baking, and crafting …

The tree was still crooked. "A little to the left, I think." Kate stood with her hands on her hips. "No, maybe more to the right."

Will lay under the tree trying to adjust it in the stand. "Katie! Which left? Which right? I can't see what you're doing."

"Toward the stairs?" Kate waited to see how that worked. "Yes! That's the right way. It looks straight from the front door."

"What about from the dining room?" Will's voice came muffled from under the bushy bottom of the pine tree.

Kate moved into the dining room, twisting her mouth. "Oh, it needs to go more toward the back of the house. Just a little more."

"I can only screw this in so far without it tipping the tree stand." He sounded impatient.

"Well, stop there and let me see how it looks from the entry." Kate considered the tree. It was beautiful, but it wasn't perfect. With the sun shining through the branches, it had a little curvature of the trunk. Will was trying his best. "By the time it's decorated, it will look great."

"It doesn't already look great?" Will crawled out from under the tree. "What's wrong with it? For the wedding, I want it perfect." He stood next to Kate and gazed at the tree. "Oh. The trunk isn't exactly straight, is it?"

Kate shrugged. "Not exactly, but we can cover any issues with decorations, lights, and other ornaments. Resist the urge to go get the level, Mr. Engineer. It's fine."

"But …"

"Pretend you're an innkeeper and not an engineer. It will work just fine. We could always tie it to the stairs if you're afraid it will fall down." Kate laughed. "Darling, I'm satisfied."

"But you shouldn't have to settle on okay versus perfect. I was sure that trunk was straight in the woods." Will rubbed his hair into spikes then smoothed it back down. Then he scrubbed the pine sap in his beard stubble. "It's okay for now, I guess." He reached for her. "I want everything to be perfect for when we say, 'I do'."

"We don't need a fancy wedding for that. As long as you are there with a minister and a marriage license, it will be all I need to make our wedding perfect." Kate leaned in and kissed him. "The decorations for the tree are in the attic."

Will sighed. "Should I go ahead and put the lights on before our guests arrive?"

"That would probably move things along. I bought

LED lights, so we don't have to worry about hot bulbs." Kate checked the time. Two o'clock. One hour until guests arrive. "I need to mix another batch of cookie dough to add to the ones already in the refrigerator."

"You mix the cookies, and I'll light up the tree." Will held her close and kissed her lips. "I love you, Katie."

"I love you, Will Bell." After another hug, she hurried to the kitchen.

As she measured ingredients into her mixing bowl, Kate's mind went back to the message a guest had given her in November. A twelve-year-old boy had become stuck in the Bell Witch Cave. After his rescue, young Murray began having nightmares and believed the Bell Witch was speaking to him.

Adams had gained fame for an event that began in 1817. An evil entity bothered the Bell family, pulling off sheets, slapping the daughter, and turning the household upside down. The stories drew many overnight visitors whom the Bell family fed and bedded over several years. The entity became known as the Bell Witch who somehow attended and then repeated the sermons from all the local churches at the Bells' home. Even Andrew Jackson visited. His remark upon leaving was that he'd rather fight the British again than to spend another night with the Bell Witch! Eventually, the family patriarch, John, was poisoned and died. His death was officially attributed to the Witch, also known as Kate's Bell Witch, referring to an old woman named Kate in the community who reportedly had a grudge against John Bell.

Before he left in early November, young Murray told Kate that the Bell Witch told him that Kate should not marry into the Bell family. Will's family often said 'no relation' after their last name, but Kate had done some research into the family tree. She believed they were, in fact, members of the infamous Bell family. *Why would I be warned against marrying Will Bell?*

Kate startled when Will's arms surrounded her.

"Hey, it's only me." Will kissed her neck. "I got the lights on the tree. Where were you?"

Kate wasn't sure she should even tell Will about the message Murray had relayed to her. "I was thinking about Murray MacGowan and hoping he and his family are doing well."

Will hugged her tight and snuggled into her neck. "Oh, you need to let that weekend go. A murder mystery dinner. Amid the death of Old Murray MacGowan, young Murray getting stuck in the cave, and people being arrested and in the hospital, we should never do that again."

"For sure."

The doorbell rang, interrupting the moment. "Finish what you're doing, Katie. I'll get the door." Will hugged her, then ran off to the foyer.

Kate finished the spicy speculaas dough. Speculaas was her favorite cookie. It was a tradition in the Netherlands and Germany. She breathed in the smell of spices which to her was the smell of Christmas and wrapped the dough in plastic wrap. Kate could buy windmill cookies at the store, but they were never as good as homemade. She added it to the refrigerator with the sugar cookie and gingerbread dough. Then she washed her hands, filled the mixing bowl with water, and took off her apron before heading to the foyer.

Will jogged into the foyer and grinned at the tree. The lights among the green boughs looked festive even without the decorations. Christmas was his favorite holiday. Having the wedding two days before the 25th was a bonus for him. And he couldn't wait to claim Katie as his own wife always. His best Christmas present ever. Everything was going well except for that job.

He opened the door. "Hello, I'm Will Bell, Katie's fiancé."

The family standing on the front porch included twin girls with long blonde braids. The girls appeared to be about ten years old or so.

"Hi, I'm Jordan Martin. This is my wife Ellen and the girls Joy and Faith."

"Welcome, come in." Will stepped inside and held the door for the Martins.

The girls cried out and ran to look at the tree.

Katie joined them. "Hi, I'm Kate."

"It's so good to meet you." Ellen Martin held out her hands to Kate. "You are providing the best Christmas gift for us. We are being stationed in Germany with the military. Our twelve-year-old girls are having a hard time with the move, in addition to us not decorating for Christmas. This will be a good weekend to transition."

"The movers are packing us up while we're here. I hope it's okay to put presents under your tree tonight for the girls." Jordan whispered the last bit.

"That would be great." Katie grinned.

Will stepped over to his Katie and draped his arm around her shoulders.

"You're in rooms numbered two and three. I assume the girls are in one room and parents in the other."

Ellen nodded. "Just like at home."

Katie handed them a packet with keys to their rooms and the front door. She also had included gift cards for Adams Station BBQ for lunch on Saturday. A map of the area was also enclosed. "Will's mom plans to make sequined ornaments with you, and I have three types of cookies to roll out, cut, bake, and then decorate. Plus, we're decorating the tree this evening."

Jordan sniffed the air. "What is that wonderful aroma?"

"Beef stew and cornbread will be ready about five o'clock. Our other guests should be here shortly."

Will stepped forward. "Relax, enjoy the Christmas activities, and let us know how we can help."

One of the girls whispered in her mother's ear.

"Yes, up the stairs." The girls headed up together. "We'll get settled and return to work on the tree."

Katie nodded. He could feel her shoulders relax as the Martins disappeared up the stairs.

"Are you okay?" Will took her hands. "You were quite tense."

"Remember, we're evaluating in January. I do get tense meeting new people and wondering what crazy thing will go wrong each weekend." Katie kissed him. "I'll be fine. I love you."

Will never tired of hearing her say those three magic words. They made his heart swell with love for her. They'd been friends forever. Soon they'd be husband and wife as well. He just hoped he hadn't jinxed his marriage before it even began by opening that shady contract deal.

The front door crashed open as another family spilled into the foyer.

"Sorry about that. It gave easier than I expected." The man pulled his wife and sons in with him. "Matthias Green." He stuck out a hand and shook Katie and Will's hands in turn.

The wife was a dark redhead with happy freckles. "I'm Jenny, this is Trevor and Tyler." She pointed to the boys, who looked close in age. "Trevor is ten and Tyler is nine."

Katie handed them their packet of important papers and keys. "You're in rooms numbered four and five. The other family just arrived as well and are in two and three. Dinner is at five o'clock."

Will stepped forward. "Can I help with your luggage?"

Matthias frowned. "It's only two nights. This bag is all we need."

As the Green family headed upstairs, Will leaned over and whispered in Katie's ear. "The Martins had a large bag for each person."

"They're also on their way to Europe after this." Katie headed for the kitchen.

She only made it to the sitting room when the sound of shattering glass split the silence.

Chapter 4

Two families for Christmas …

The shattering glass set Will in motion. He took the stairs by twos to discover the cause of the sound. Katie wasn't far behind.

When they arrived, room three was open. Matthias and Jenny Green with their boys looked on in horror. The twin girls were crying. Their father, Jordan, was yelling at them, and their mom, Ellen, was trying to comfort them. The antique mirror that hung over the vanity was in a million pieces.

"I told you not to bring that ball!" Jordan waved his hands in the air. "Look what you've done. I'm going to have to buy Miss Kate a new antique mirror."

A hard red rubber ball sat in front of the mirror frame among all the shattered glass on the vanity.

"Joy took it out of the suitcase and wouldn't give it back. Then she threw it out of my reach, and it hit the mirror." Faith crossed her arms. "This is not my fault."

Joy yanked Faith's braids.

"Ouch!" Faith grabbed Joy's braids and twisted

them.

Joy yowled like a coon dog.

Katie just stared at the broken mirror. "Seven years bad luck."

Will held her to him. "That's just superstition. It will be okay. We'll get another one from Clark's Antiques."

She looked up at him with tears spilling over her lashes.

"Sweetheart, it's just an accident. Nothing more." Will guided her out of the room to regain her composure.

"I need to tell you something." Katie wiped her face with her hands.

"Save it for later."

Jordan approached them. "I'm sorry for the destruction of your mirror. How much would it cost to replace?"

"I don't know. I'd have to check with the local antique shop." Will could tell Katie was struggling to stop the tears.

"I'm sorry." She scooted to her room and closed herself inside.

"Man, I'm more than sorry about that." Jordan looked to Will with a sad face. "How can I help?"

Will attempted a smile. "Our wedding is on the twenty-third. Things are becoming a little tense as we prepare the house. I'll look into replacing the mirror." He grabbed the broom and dustpan from the hall closet.

Ellen Martin took the broom from Will. "That's something we can do, right girls? Let us clean it up. It's the least we can do."

Will tried to smile. "Okay. Jordan, why don't we

go over to Clark's now? We have an hour and a half until dinner. While we're gone, the rest of you can put decorations on the tree. They're in the boxes surrounding it." He whispered. "Some of them are antiques from Katie's great-grandmother."

Ellen nodded. "Message received. Girls, be very careful with the ornaments."

Jenny Green corralled her boys. "That goes double for you two troublemakers."

Will tapped on Katie's door. "Jordan and I are headed over to Clark's. I'll try to find a comparable mirror or put Clark on the search for one. I love you, Katie. It will be okay."

A muffled reply made Will cringe inside. All he could do to fix the situation was to buy another mirror. "Jordan, grab the mirror frame, so we know what size we need."

Kate heard her guests go down the stairs not long after Will left for Clark's. She washed her face and re-tied her ponytail. She still wanted to cry. Whenever she'd stayed at Aunt Katharine's, she'd stayed in room three. That mirror was the one she used to pretend to put on makeup. It was the one in which she had conversations with her own reflection. She'd also pretended to kiss Will – Billy then – in that mirror. Like her childhood in Adams, the mirror was gone. It'd be too embarrassing to explain why she held sentimentality over a mirror.

She dabbed on some makeup to cover the redness

in her face. She sighed. Makeup didn't really help, but it helped her put on that brave face anyway. She needed to make cornbread to go with the stew. She'd skirt around the tree, and their guests, as best as she could.

When Kate reached the bottom of the stairs, she gasped. The tree was beautiful. The LED lights illuminated the ornaments from a century ago, combined with newer plastic ones. "It looks beautiful." Her voice came out croaky. She cleared her throat, and her guests looked at her. "You're doing a great job."

Trevor came to her holding one of the precious antique ornaments. "Is there a story with this ornament? It looks older than most of the others."

Kate took the ornament and looked at it. "Yes. This ornament is from the late 1800s, after the Civil War. See the American flag in the background with the family by the tree? It's one of the oldest ones I have from my family."

Tyler joined his brother looking at the glass ball. "Don't give it to those girls then unless you want them to break it."

An uproar of crying and yelling from the children returned.

Kate placed the ornament at the top of the tree, as far as she could reach. She'd get Will to put it higher when he returned. *I should have sorted out the precious ornaments in preparation for children decorating the tree.*

"I'll go finish supper." She hurried away from the mayhem to the relative peace of the kitchen.

Will and Jordan returned at 4:45 with a new mirror. The tree was beautiful from the floor to about five feet. The upper branches were bare.

"Katie, we're back!" Will called out to her. She probably couldn't hear him over the Christmas music playing on the intercom system.

Haggling with Clark was exhausting as always. It shouldn't have taken that long to buy a mirror. They carried it upstairs and mounted it on the vanity. It wasn't a perfect match, but it was close enough for now.

"Thanks for taking me with you to pick out the mirror. I'll impress my girls on how delicate and expensive some things are. That Clark is a real character, isn't he?" Jordan shook Will's hand.

"Ever since I've known him." Will agreed. "Katie planned supper for five o'clock. You have just got time to wash up." Will went down the stairs to the kitchen.

"Will, I didn't hear you come in. I have the music on, so I couldn't hear any problems with decorating the tree." Kate looked up into his face. "I practiced putting on make-up and kissing in that mirror."

"When you were ten? Who are you and what have you done with my sweet, innocent Katie?" Will laughed and spun her around. "I wish I'd known that then. I wish a lot of things had been different." He wrapped her in his arms. "We can replace the mirror in the frame later."

The cuckoo sounded five times.

"No time for what-ifs now." She kissed him. "Ring the dinner bell, and I'll serve the food."

Katie escaped his grasp and opened the Crock-Pot.

The wonderful aroma of beef stew escaped.

"Oh, that is the most amazing smell." Will closed his eyes and reveled in the aroma of the stew and the closeness of his bride-to-be. "You are the best cook. I love you."

Katie swatted him with a dish towel. "Go ring the bell."

Will reluctantly left the kitchen for the foyer and the antique dinner bell from, where else, Clark's Antiques. He rang it heartily and footsteps sounded from all over the second floor. Even Beebe, the white lab he'd given Katie at their engagement, howled at the summons. The four children appeared first, followed by their respective adults.

Katie served the stew to the children first, then to the adults. She brought out two baskets of cornbread. Will took drink orders for iced tea, coffee, milk, and hot chocolate.

Once everyone had been served, Katie asked, "Do you have everything you need?"

Universal agreement gave Katie and Will the chance to retire to the kitchen for their meal. Just as they finished the prayer over the food, Beebe began barking ferociously. Will jumped to his feet and, following the sound, ran up the stairs to Katie's bedroom.

The door stood wide open.

Chapter 5

The first two disruptions …

Kate ran up the stairs behind Will. After he barged into her room, she heard a heavy thud. *Oh no! What happened?*

When she flipped the light switch on, Will was flat on his back on the floor. No wonder since the floor was littered with pearls. A glance at her dress confirmed her fears. Her necklace had been cut and spilled. She kneeled on the floor beside Will.

"Are you hurt?" Kate touched his shoulder.

Will, stunned by the fall, sat up cautiously. "Just a little dazed. Nothing permanent."

She kissed him and began gathering the pearls into her empty water glass.

After watching her for a moment, Will helped scoop up the precious gems into the glass.

When the glass was full, Kate found a small basket in which to gather more round beads. She crept under the bed and found more pearls. *Why would anyone break into my room and break my necklace? Is this about interrupting the wedding? Or is it a warning of some kind?* Overwhelmed by the task and its significance, she crawled back out from under the bed and leaned against it.

"Who was in my room?" Kate dropped her head back against the bed.

"The lock's been broken. It was someone Beebe didn't know or didn't like." Will sank down beside her and took her hand. "We can get them restrung in time for the wedding."

Kate sighed. "No, it takes time to re-string pearls. They are supposed to be hand-knotted between each pearl. Clearly these were not." Tears leaked down her cheeks. "So, it begins. Will, how do we survive until the new year."

Will squeezed her hand. "I plan to marry you on the twenty-third, regardless of whatever craziness happens between now and then."

"Why does there have to be craziness?" Kate leaned over onto Will's shoulder. "What have we done to gain the attention of people who wish to harm us?"

"I don't know, Katie." He wrapped an arm around her shoulders and pulled her to him. "Just remember that I love you, no matter what."

"I guess I need to tend to our guests. Could you take Beebe out? I don't need him eating my pearls. My father gave these to me." Kate sniffed. She stood and grabbed a tissue.

"Of course, whatever you need." Will stood and wrapped her in his arms. "Don't forget…"

"I love you and you love me. I know. Who is trying to make us afraid?" Kate wiped her eyes.

"Don't know. We'll find out. I'll take another look

on the floor for any pearls we may have missed before I let Beebe out of his crate." He leaned down and kissed her. "You let me into the inner sanctum, your bedroom."

Kate laughed. "Someone else got in before you, it seems."

A knock on the bedroom door pulled Kate's attention away from Will.

Jordan Martin was at the door. "Excuse me, Ms. Kate? Is everything okay? We're done with the stew and muffins. Is there anything we can do to help? Also, the kids are wondering if there's dessert."

"Of course, there most definitely is dessert. It wouldn't be Christmas without dessert." Kate struggled out of Will's arms and headed out of the bedroom and down the stairs.

Will slumped down onto the bed. Did this have anything to do with the contract he'd accepted? The one for a bunker for a crime family operating in the southeast area of the USA? What had he done, doubting that God would provide for them? How could he get out of accepting the contract?

He noticed a couple more pearls below the window against the woodwork. It was silly to think the mob would break Katie's pearl necklace. Wasn't it? Or was it a warning that they could get into Katie's bedroom and destroy something precious, even his Katie? He needed to warn her about the danger in which he'd placed them, even though he'd been sworn to secrecy.

Excited voices grabbed his attention. Katie needed his help, so he placed the two additional pearls into the basket.

"I bet you need to go out, Beebe." Will grabbed his leash to keep the white lab from upsetting the Christmas tree and jumping on the children on the journey from Katie's room to the backyard. "Come on. Thanks for alerting us to the intruder. Good dog."

When Will opened the crate, Beebe jumped up onto Will, knocking him onto the bed.

"Dude, I'm not allowed in Katie's bed for a couple more weeks."

Will stretched and shoved the dog off the bed. A piece of paper crinkled under his touch on the pillow. He pulled it to him and read the warning: "DON'T MARRY WILL BELL!"

Will took the paper and slipped it into his shirt pocket. "Who doesn't want Katie to marry me?" He felt a stab in his heart. Beebe whined. "It's okay, guy. Let's go out."

Will raced down the stairs and through the dining room and kitchen with the white Labrador to the backyard.

"There's a dog! Dad, there's a dog here!" Children's voices rejoiced at seeing Beebe race through the room. "Can we pet him?"

Beebe didn't stop for the kids on his way through the kitchen and out into the yard. Will waved as he ran past. Once he unhooked Beebe in the backyard, Will hurried back into the kitchen.

Katie walked into the kitchen from the dining room. "What was that about?"

"Just taking the dog out. By the way, I heard on the

radio in the truck that a winter storm is heading this way. It's supposed to arrive in the morning sometime." Will grabbed a fork and took a bite of the coconut cake on the counter. "Oh, Katie-girl, this is amazing. Mom will want your recipe."

"I also made a jam cake. Do you need a plate, perhaps, to have a slice of each?" Katie leaned against the counter with her arms crossed. "Pretty sure the state health department wouldn't want you eating it from the whole cake with a fork."

Will had his fork poised to get another bite. He laughed. "You're probably right. May I have a plate and actual slices of cake?"

"Of course." Katie sliced the cakes and loaded a slice of each onto a plate. She chuckled as she placed the plate on the table. "Have a seat."

"Message received. Act civil." Will saluted and sat in a kitchen chair at the table. "I found two more pearls below the window."

Katie shook her head. "I don't want to talk about that now. Can I get a new lock on that door by tonight?"

"Absolutely. I bought extras from that restoration site when we put the new locks on all the doors in August." He took a bite of the jam cake on his plate. "Oh, so good, too. Tastes like Christmas."

Katie gave him a guarded smile. "I'm glad you're enjoying it."

Children entered the kitchen with stacks of plates. "Here, Ms. Kate. We loved the cake and the dinner. Thank you. We're going to finish decorating the tree."

"Thanks. I appreciate your help." Katie brightened and gave them a real smile, taking the plates from the girls and then the boys. "Does Mr. Will need to tend to the fire?"

The children looked at one another for an answer then shrugged.

"I'll have him check it."

"Can we go out into the yard with the dog?" Tyler asked.

Katie looked to Will for help. "What do you think? Is Beebe too wild for children right now?"

Will looked outside. It was already dark.

"If it's okay with your parents, maybe you can play with him tomorrow when it's light outside." Will gave them a wink, which made them all laugh.

"Okay." The chorus of children's voices warmed his heart. They ran off together to the dining room or foyer.

Will laughed to himself about how readily they took his response. *Now if they'd been our kids, we would have heard, "Aww. It's not that late."*

"Good job, Mr. Will." Kate nodded. "You're a natural."

"Thank you, ma'am."

Kate sighed. "Who would want to break my pearl necklace? How did they get in? Are they still here?"

"Thought you didn't want to talk about it." Will took another bite of cake.

"I don't. I just need to know that we'll be safe tonight, me, you, and our guests."

Will swallowed the bite. "Darling, we don't know for sure, but I'd bet whoever is long gone once Beebe started barking and yelping."

Katie had that look she got when things were unsettled, like a thunderstorm behind her eyes.

"Don't worry. I'll throw a new log on the fire, then

I'll put a new lock on your bedroom door. Should I also lock all the doors and set the alarm?" Will took another bite.

"Don't set the alarm until our guests have turned in for the night. It'd be just like one of our young guests to open the front door to see what happens." Katie took his left hand since the right hand was busy shoveling cake.

"I'll go get my sleeping bag. I can sleep in front of the fire tonight." Will finished off the cake, then he drew her hand to his lips. "I love you. Everything will be okay."

He let Beebe in and took him back to Katie's bedroom. He checked the doors and windows. All secure. Then he went out the kitchen door to grab his sleeping bag from the converted garage.

At the bottom of the dark steps from the kitchen, a hand reached out of the gloom and grabbed his arm. "Good evening, Mr. Bell. Our boss wants to discuss his project."

Another man grabbed his other arm. "He's been waiting for you. He doesn't like to be kept waiting."

Will let them 'escort' him to the garage. When he stepped inside, a rough-looking man with scars on his face and tattoos up and down his arms sat at the desk with his biker boots propped up on it.

"Nice of you to join us. You can call me Demeter. Sit."

The henchmen shoved Will into the chair on the opposite side of the desk.

"What's this about? I haven't even started the project. No one knows about it. I haven't even read it in detail." Will tried to stay calm.

"Relax, dude. This is just a friendly conversation. Thought you'd like to meet who you're working for." Demeter spit tobacco into a fast-food drink cup. "We need this bunker by Christmas. It needs air circulation from outside, heat and air unnecessary. Just livable in case we have to go underground."

The two henchmen laughed. "Good one, boss."

"How did you know I opened the attachment file and where to find me?" Will rubbed his damp palms on his jeans.

"Geo tag. Sent me your location and info as soon as you opened the file." Demeter moved his boots from the desk and stood. "Christmas. Got it? Hear you're getting married then. I'd hate to be the one to ruin the nuptials."

"Yeah, that Katie is one sweet chica." One of the henchmen laughed and ribbed the other.

"Leave Katie out of it." Will's anger burned but striking out against these three would be dangerous for Katie. "I can only do what I can do, Demeter. I'll do my best to have it done by Christmas."

Demeter nodded his head. He pulled on a black leather biker jacket. "We'll leave you in peace … for now." He opened the garage door with the remote on Will's desk.

Three Harley-Davidson motorcycles stood on the driveway. The men mounted and rode away in a whirl of sound and fury.

Will closed the door with the remote and collapsed into his desk chair. Adrenaline had him shaking. *What have I done? I've put us in jeopardy.*

Chapter 6

Locks and breakfast …

Will was rolling up the sleeping bag when the front door opened, and the security system chimed.

"Hello!" Will recognized his mom's voice. "Oh, what a great-looking tree. Ooh, presents, too."

"I'm in the living room, Mom." He stashed the bag behind a chair.

"You're not even married, and you're already relegated to the couch? Tsk. Don't you have a bed in the garage?" She set her craft box on the couch. "What did you do to end up in the doghouse?"

"I'm not in the doghouse. I'm just trying to keep everyone safe. We had an intruder break into Katie's room during dinner. Whoever it was broke her pearl necklace that she had planned to wear for the wedding." He refused to mention the biker gang incident to his mom.

"Oh, no. Was anyone hurt?" She reached out and hugged him.

"No, we only knew it happened because Beebe

started barking.

"So glad you got that dog. We'll need to see about restringing those pearls then. I know someone to call." Mom rummaged through her tote bag and found her phone. "Where's Katie?"

"In the kitchen, I suppose." Will really hoped that's where she was. Now he was afraid of retribution from the biker gang. He really should not have opened that document.

He walked through the downstairs, checking windows and doors. Once satisfied that the house was secure, he slipped into the kitchen.

"Good morning, sweetheart." Will hugged Katie and gave her a smooch on the cheek since his mom was there too. "I need to check on a few things in the office."

"Not a problem. Mom is here to do the crafts, and I'll do the cookies once we've had breakfast." Katie looked at him. "Are you okay? You seem tense."

"After the intruder last night? You don't seem tense enough." That sounded critical, and he didn't need to be. "I'm sorry. That came out wrong."

"Grab a cup of coffee, at least." Katie handed him a mug and gave him a kiss on his cheek. "It's okay. I'm just compartmentalizing it this morning."

Will nodded, poured a cup of coffee, and escaped the concerned interrogation of the ladies. If he could help it, neither one would know about his late evening visitors.

Kate nodded to Maddy, Will's mom, as she entered the kitchen with her craft box.

"Does he seem strange to you this morning?" Maddy quirked an eyebrow. "Almost like he has a secret he's not sharing."

Pulling the breakfast casserole from the oven, Kate nodded. "I agree. Something's definitely off with him today. Did he tell you about our intruder and my pearls? I need to go up in the light of day to see if we missed any of them."

"I can do that while you're setting breakfast on the table. Will said he replaced your lock. Can I have the key?" Maddy held out her hand. "Should I let Beebe out? That storm is getting closer."

Kate cut the casserole into serving sizes. "Not right now. He's been out. I don't want him in the middle of cookies and sequins with four children."

"That's wise. Do you know how many pearls you had?" Maddy grabbed a container with a lid. "Doesn't matter. I know someone who has experience stringing pearls the correct way."

Kate waved her on. "Mine were subpar in that regard. While you're upstairs, could you knock on rooms two and four and tell them breakfast is served?"

Maddy nodded and scurried about her tasks.

Kate slumped into a chair. She hadn't slept a wink. The sounds of children on the stairs motivated her to finish setting the food on the table.

"Hey, not fair. The girls got gifts under the tree, but we don't." One of the boys' voices rang out loud and clear.

"Besides, it's not Christmas yet." Another Green son's voice.

Kate watched as Jenny Green soothed her sons' hurt feelings. Soon they were engrossed in casserole, fruit, and juice.

"Wow! I hope wisdom comes with parenthood." Kate patted Jenny on the shoulder.

"Nope, it's on-the-job training. Did I hear you and Will are getting married soon?"

Kate nodded. "The twenty-third, if all goes well."

"Congratulations! Will seems like a great guy. He has handled the kids well while they were decorating the tree yesterday."

"Mr. Will is going to help us play with the dog. What's his name?" Trevor scratched his head. "BeeBee, CeeCee, DeeDee?"

"Beebe." Kate smiled. Life was so simple for them. Do what Mom and Dad say. Eat when there's food. Go wherever they're told to go.

The girls entered the dining room. "There are presents under the tree!"

The boys sulked.

"We're moving to Germany, so we're having Christmas early." One of the twins sat down next to Tyler, the younger boy. "What did you ask Santa for?"

"We haven't seen Santa yet." Tyler hung his head. "I want a Lego set."

Kate made sure all the food was on the table, then she retired to the kitchen.

Maddy held up a carousel horse ornament full of sequins and beads. "What do you think?"

"Wow! It's beautiful. Do you think the kids can do that?"

"Probably not." Maddy held up an apple and a star. "These are easier for the kids. The adults can do the horses and poinsettias.”

Kate nodded. “Sounds good. One family can cut out cookies while the other makes ornaments. I guess we’ll all be decorating cookies after lunch.”

“You’re doing a fine job, Katie. Relax. Why don’t you go speak to Will?” Maddy nodded toward the kitchen door. “Take him some breakfast. Everything’s under control here.”

Kate prepared a plate and hurried through the falling sleet, stinging her face and clinging to her hair. When she reached the door and grabbed the doorknob, it was locked. *Why is it locked?* She knocked. Will’s face appeared at the window. He quickly undid three additional locks that weren’t on the door before. The door flew open, and Will grabbed her arm and pulled her in.

“Katie, get in out of the weather. Thank you for breakfast, but I’d have come back when I got hungry.” While he jabbered, he redid the locks and pulled the curtain over the window in the door.

“What’s happening here, Will? Are you okay? When did you start securing the door?” Alarms went off inside her mind and body. Adrenaline flooded her senses. She set the plate on his desk and sat down in the chair in front of it. She tried to calm her heart. “What’s wrong?”

Will kneeled down beside her. “I can’t tell you, but it’s very dangerous. The less you know, the better for you.”

“Don’t you know by now that if it threatens you, it threatens me? Whatever danger you face, I stand beside you.” She took his hand. “You can tell me anything. Unless it involves breaking up with me, I’ll be here with you."

Will gave her a half smile and winked at her. "I love you too. I made a big mistake yesterday." He stood up from the cold concrete floor and sat on the front edge of his desk. "My life is in danger, and so is yours, if I don't fulfill a contract I opened from an email."

"Sounds odd. How did this contract put us in danger? I have many questions." Kate began to shake. Her staccato heartbeat warned her to relax. "How would these folks know if you told me anything?"

Will's eyes lit up with understanding. He scribbled on a notepad and handed it to her.

Kate read the one word written there: BUG? She nodded to him. "You should come back to the house. For one thing, it's warmer. For another, you can get a hot breakfast. What I brought is cold by now. I'm due to lead cookie making in just a few minutes."

He nodded with a sad grimace. "I love you."

"I know. Come on." She picked up the plate and headed out the door after undoing all the locksets.

Once outside the office, Will secured the door.

"What happened to make you put more locks on that door? Why are you locking yourself in?" Kate held his arm as they walked the ever-icier concrete walkway to the kitchen. Icicles hung from the rail on the steps to the kitchen.

"Three men met me in my office after dinner last night. The project is for an illegal … thing. They threatened your life if I don't complete the contract by Christmas."

He spoke so fast she didn't quite catch all of his words. She turned on the icy steps and looked into his brown eyes. "You mean between now and the wedding?"

He nodded slowly.

"It would take that long just to get the permits …"

He closed his eyes and nodded.

"Oh, Will! You could lose your license or your freedom to do a project off the books."

"Oh, I know."

The door flew open. Maddy gasped. "You two need to get in here. The weather's horrible, and your guests are ready to craft and bake." She looked back and forth between them. "What's going on? Is something wrong?"

"You could say that." Kate slipped as she turned to enter the house.

Will caught her but not the plate she was carrying. It smashed into pieces on the icy concrete steps.

"Oh, no!" With Will's recounting of a gang expecting the impossible, the spilled pearl necklace, an intruder, the shattered mirror, and now the broken plate, Kate began to tear up. Her insides were as shattered as the plate on the concrete.

Once Will set her down, Maddy helped her into the house. "Don't worry about the plate. I'll clean it up. You can always buy more plates. But …"

"There's only one Katie. Right, Mom?" Will finished her sentence. "I couldn't bear to lose you again."

They all came inside to children and their mayhem. Maddy gathered the broom and dustpan from the broom closet and went back out to sweep up the mess.

Kate put her hands on his shoulders. "I can't lose you either. Maybe you should speak with Andy, off the record."

"Not sure what I'd have to tell him can be 'off the record'." Will opened the door for his mom.

A shattering thud overwhelmed the other noises in the house. Beebe came running into the kitchen and hid behind Kate.

"What now?"

Chapter 7

Cookies and crafts …

Will ran to the foyer to find the tree on the floor with some ornaments broken and others rolling around on the floor. Four children stood with downcast faces.

"What happened?" Hearing that loud, accusatory tone again in his question, Will lowered his voice and asked again. "What caused the tree to fall over?"

In unison, the four shrugged. Beebe raced through the foyer and up the stairs, whining at Katie's bedroom door.

"Oh, no!" Katie's voice. She had come in from the kitchen, drying her hands on her apron.

Will winced. He didn't need to add any more tension to the situation. It was hard enough learning how to run a bed and breakfast without adding a criminal gang element to the mix.

She kneeled on the floor next to a broken antique ornament. When she closed her eyes, tears flowed onto her cheeks. Time seemed to stand still.

Will rushed to her and wrapped his arms around her.

Katie sighed. "It's okay. They're only things. You and me. That's what matters most."

His heart seemed to break at her grief.

"It's just another letting go of my family, Will. I feel so alone when these keepsakes inevitably break." She sniffled and wiped her tears with her hand.

The water from the tree stand puddled closer to where she kneeled. Will jumped up and raced for a towel to clean it up. When he returned, Jordan Martin had the broom from upstairs at work sweeping up the broken glass. Matthias Green had righted the tree, and the children were picking up the unbroken ornaments from the floor and adding them back onto the tree. Jenny Green grabbed the towel from Will and began blotting up water.

Katie drifted up the stairs. Will heard Katie's bedroom door close. Will took the stairs two at a time and tried the doorknob. Locked, as always.

"Katie. Let me in, sweetheart. Let me help."

"Get out half the cookie dough from the fridge. The mom of one family can start with that. Maddy can start the ornaments with the other family. I need to get myself back in order." After a pause, she added, "I love you."

Kate heard Will retreat down the stairs. She wanted desperately to let him in but breaking that barrier would make putting it back up for three weeks that much harder. Honestly, she needed to spend a few minutes in prayer, otherwise she might not make it through the day between the guests and the mysterious project Will had undertaken.

She took her mom's Bible from her nightstand and opened it to Luke 1. She began reading. When she got to verse 26, the word 'Mary' was written in her mom's handwriting. Below it was written 'Matthew 1:18'. Kate turned the crinkly old pages to Matthew. Next to verse 18 was written 'Joseph' and 'Luke 2:1.' These were the verses for the nativity set!

Kate jumped up from the bed and took the Bible to her desk. She grabbed a journal and began writing down the verses for each of the figures. Before long, she had reproduced her mom's nativity info, and she felt better about everything. God was in control, no matter how crazy things seemed.

Nativity Verses

Mary	Luke 1:26-38
Joseph	Matthew 1:18-25
Manger, animals	Luke 2:4-7
Shepherds, sheep	Luke 2:8, 15-20
Angels	Luke 2:9-14
Kings	Matthew 2:1-12

A tap on the door refocused her attention.

"Yes?" Kate stood and opened the door.

"Katie, the cookies are ready to go into the oven. Do you want to do that?" Maddy's voice made Kate smile.

"Are the families ready to change activities?" Kate opened the door to Maddy's smiling face.

"The ornaments are taking longer for the kids, well, for the adults too. I think my family is ready to do something else."

"I'll be right down. Take a look at this." Kate

handed her the journal with the nativity verse list. "Mom would read these scriptures as we placed the nativity pieces. I found the information in her Bible."

"Your mom was pretty special, y'know." Maddy handed the journal back. "Sounds just like her. I still miss her."

Kate checked her hair and wiped her face with a damp wash cloth. "I do, too. Especially at Christmas. Dad didn't do any Christmas traditions." She walked into the hall with Maddy then closed and locked her door. "Thank you for remembering her."

Maddy pulled her into a hug. "Of course, I can't replace her, but I can fill a mom's role for you. I love you, Katie."

"I love you, too." Kate kissed her cheek.

Christmas music filled the house. Kate breathed in the smells and sounds of Christmas.

"I turned on your music. I hope that was okay."

Kate hugged her. "It's perfect. I needed that."

When they reached the foyer, Will was tying the tree to the stairs. The children were gathered around watching him.

"I've never seen someone tie a tree to the steps." One of the twins looked on with a skeptic's face. "Guess it's a good idea since it fell down."

"Are you sure you didn't do something to make it fall?" One of the boys sneered at the girls.

"I bet they did something to make it fall." The second boy wagged a finger at the twins.

"Mom!" the girls cried out.

Maddy stepped in. "Ladies, why don't we decorate ornaments, and the boys can roll out cookies now?"

The children scattered to the kitchen and dining

room for the next activity. Maddy followed them.

Kate stayed to speak to Will. "Thank you for fixing the tree." Tears spilled over. "I love you. I appreciate all you do to help us have a good future together. I'm with you, no matter what." She stretched onto tiptoes to kiss his cheek.

Will pointed to the ceiling. On the ceiling over the base of the stairs hung a bunch of mistletoe. He hugged her and moved her under the greenery. Then he gave her another mistletoe kiss.

Will came in from the garage at noon, slipping and sliding so much on the icy walk that he ended up walking in the crunchy grass. Careful not to fall on the steps, he held onto the rail until he could step into the house.

The aromas of vanilla, ginger, and spice filled the kitchen.

"That smells just like Christmas." He took a deep breath and enjoyed it.

Mom and Katie sat at the kitchen table drinking coffee.

"Grab a cup. Pizza is being delivered soon." Katie's smile made his heart beat faster.

"Where are our guests?" He poured a cup of coffee and sipped it black.

"They went to Springfield for pizza. Where do you think I got the idea to order one?" Mom grinned. "Those kids needed to get out of the house. We'll decorate cookies when they return."

"How are the ornaments coming?" Will sat down at the table with the ladies.

"They'll need another session before they're done. Maybe more." Mom put her hand over her face. "Guess I planned too big."

"Well, better more than not enough." Will stood when the doorbell rang.

Kate laughed. "Guess that's right. I'm exhausted."

"Go get the pizza, Billy. I already paid for it." Mom held Katie's hand. "Be sure you tip the delivery guy. The roads are a mess."

After pizza and the return of the families, decorating cookies began for the first bakers of the day.

Kate began her instructions for squeezing icing out of a bag. "You want to hold the icing in your hand. When you press on the icing, it will come out of the tip you put on the bag. Any questions?"

Green and red icing flowed freely. Despite her instructions, icing was everywhere. The angel, Santa, holly, and candle cookies weren't anywhere near as pretty as the ones at Sarah's Bakery, but the children thought they were beautiful and tasty.

The first family to work on ornaments continued putting sequins into the empty places on them. They swapped places partway through the afternoon with a similar effect.

By then, the sleet had turned to snow, the fluffy kind that seemed to fall in balls.

While Kate cleaned up the cookie making mess,

Jenny Green came into the kitchen.

"We're going back into Springfield to see a movie and have dinner. You'll be glad to have the house to yourself for a few hours."

Kate laughed. "Be careful driving on the roads."

"We will." Jenny impulsively hugged Kate. "Thank you for all you've done to make this weekend festive and enjoyable for the kids."

Will's dad Porter came to pick up Maddy because he didn't want her driving on the icy roads. Will was still in the garage, leaving Kate alone in the house. She turned off the Christmas music and scrubbed the red and green sugary food dye off the kitchen table. After packaging the cookies for each family, she stoked the fire and put on another log. The ornaments were in various stages of beautiful. The sequins reflected the firelight.

Kate wasn't hungry after licking frosting and cookie dough from her fingers all day. She decided to go up to her room and lie down for a little while. She left a note for Will. She entered the room, but Beebe didn't run to her. He was piled up in his bed. If he could sleep, maybe she could too. Surely Will's concerns were overblown.

Kate woke to a stranger hanging over her bed with a knife in his or her hand.

"Hey! Who are you and how did you get into my room?" Kate sat up quickly, and the room spun. The figure dashed out of the room and down the stairs. Kate followed. The intruder slipped down the front stairs and disappeared into the early evening darkness.

Will appeared from the kitchen. "What's going

on?"

"Someone was in my room. Beebe didn't bark at them. Maybe they hurt him." Kate hurried up the stairs to check on her white lab puppy.

She found a lethargic dog in his bed. He could barely open his eyes.

"I'll call the vet." Will had his phone out.

"Call Andy too for the intruder and the property damage." Kate pointed at her lace wedding dress, hanging in tatters from its hanger.

Will stopped dialing the phone and put his arms around her. "Who would do such a thing? Did you think you were in danger?"

She shrugged. "I don't know if they were planning to hurt me or not. They sure did a number on my dress though."

Chapter 8

Another call to the Sheriff …

From just inside the front door, Will watched for Andy Lawrence, deputy for the Robertson County Sheriff Office, to pull up. When he emerged from the vehicle, Will opened the door and yelled, "The steps are icy even though I've thrown rock salt. Be careful."

"All day long, dude. I've already busted my rear a couple of times today." Andy took the steps with precision. "What's going on? I was surprised I didn't get a call yesterday."

Will bro-hugged Andy as he entered the house. "Well, it wasn't because nothing happened."

"I'd hoped it was because nothing happened." Andy took his hat off. "What's going on?"

Will sighed. *What do I say?* "Someone is entering the house and breaking into Katie's bedroom. Whoever it is has broken Katie's pearl necklace and destroyed her wedding dress. It also appears that Beebe's been drugged. The intruder was in the room while Katie was asleep in her own bed."

"Unbelievable! Is Katie okay?" Andy hurried up

the steps to Katie's room with Will behind him.

Katie sat on the floor with Beebe's head in her lap. She stroked his head and mumbled soft syllables to him.

"The vet's coming. Andy is here, too, regarding the intruder and the dress and pearls."

When Katie looked up to Will, her eyes were filled with tears. "I just can't lose Beebe now. He's too young, and I haven't enjoyed him nearly enough yet."

Will squatted down beside her. "He's strong. The vet is on his way. It's probably just a sedative of some kind. But your dress …"

"…is just a dress ultimately. I can find something else to wear. I can't get another Beebe." She buried her face into the dog's fur. "Don't die, Beebe. Who would do this?"

"What do you remember?" Andy flipped open his notepad.

"Nothing specific. I woke up and saw a dark figure standing over me. I'm not sure why I woke up. Might have been when the dress was being slashed. Maybe it was a woman. Not very tall or big. Didn't say anything that I heard. Whoever it was didn't need to hurt my dog." Katie's eyes were angry. "Whoever did this to Beebe needs to be arrested for whatever the sheriff can charge him or her with!"

The doorbell drew Will back down the stairs. He opened the door to the vet.

"Thanks for coming out, Dr. Bradley. An intruder has drugged Beebe."

"Don't worry. Whatever they used was hopefully from a vet or pet store." Dr. Bradley carried his black medical bag and climbed the steps behind Will. "Unless they used a street drug, Beebe should be fine."

"I'm sorry you had to come on such a treacherous night, but Katie is really concerned."

"It's okay. I'm glad to help."

The men entered Katie's room. Beebe lay on Katie's lap, stiller than he ever had been. Dr. Bradley kneeled beside the dog and took his stethoscope out of his bag. He listened to his heartbeat. He used his hands to examine the dog. At one point, he parted the fur and looked closely.

"Aha, someone injected him. Unfortunately, there's not much I can do to help him here. Beebe will need to come with me back to the clinic for a couple days at least."

Katie half-gasped and half-strangled.

Dr. Bradley took her hand. "If it was going to kill him, he'd already be dead. It's probably a pet tranquilizer. I'd like to have him wake in the office just in case he needs any help."

Katie nodded. The vet picked the big limp puppy up and headed for the stairs. "Will, can you get the crate for me. Leave the toys."

Will cleared the toys from the crate and carried it downstairs, following the vet. When they reached the front door, the two guest families were just coming in.

"What's wrong with Beebe?" One of the girls reached out to pet him.

The vet moved closer to the girl's extended hand. The other children gathered around Beebe and stroked him. Dr. Bradley moved, so all the children could reach him.

"He's not feeling well, so I'm taking him to my vet office to watch over him."

Will carried the crate out to the front porch and fell on the ice onto the crate. "Be careful, Doc. It's still slick. Guess I need to throw more salt." He used the crate to struggle to his feet then picked it up.

Dr. Bradley walked down the steps and out to his SUV at the curb. Will put the crate in the back, then he helped get Beebe into it.

As the vet drove away, the sheriff's forensic team pulled up. Will walked with them to the house, avoiding the particularly icy patches, and led them indoors.

Katie stood at the bottom of the staircase. "They've roped off my room. I was able to get a nightgown, toiletries, and clothes for tomorrow. Think I could sleep in the garage?"

"No. I think you should go to Chez Bell. I can sleep by the fire tonight and rustle up some breakfast for our guests before they leave in the morning. You need a good night's sleep, darling girl." Will tapped her on the nose.

"Are you sure Maddy will be okay with that?" Katie looked up the stairs to the sounds of the forensic team tearing up her room for clues.

"Are you kidding? She'd like nothing better. I'll take you over in the truck. It will be safer than your subcompact." He pointed to the mistletoe overhead. Then he kissed her. "I want you safe. Right now, that's at Mom and Dad's."

"Okay. You win. It would feel weird to be here without Beebe anyway."

Andy descended the steps. "We won't be long. I don't guess whoever it was would know about the hidden passageways in this house."

Katie shrugged. "It's not like we advertise: 'Hidden passages to do ne'er do well things in our B&B.'"

"I'm taking Katie to Mom and Dad's to spend the night. Can you stay until I return?"

Andy nodded. "We'll be busy until then, for sure. I'll try to figure it out. Meanwhile, is there someone who's unhappy with your impending marriage?"

Katie's eyes widened. "Not that I'm aware of. Will?"

"Who knew about your pearls and dress?" Andy scanned his notepad.

"Sarah, of Sarah's Bakery. I showed her on Friday morning. She's my friend. She wouldn't do this, would she?"

Katie looked fragile to Will. "Could we do this interrogation tomorrow, after Katie's had a good night's sleep?"

Andy nodded. "Sure thing. Don't worry. We'll try to find some clues. If you think of something, write it down or text me so you don't forget."

Will picked up Katie's overnight bag and grabbed her hand. "Come on."

After the two-minute drive to Maddy and Porter's house, Kate struggled to walk up the driveway. The slush was hardening due to the falling temperatures. A cold wind blew as well.

"Hold on to my arm, and I'll pull you up the drive." Will offered a bent elbow.

Kate grabbed onto him and mostly slid up the pavement. "Be careful. I don't want black eyes in our wedding pictures."

"No worries. We've got two weeks to heal." Will laughed into the wind.

Kate scowled at his cavalier attitude, even if it was meant to lighten her mood. "Maybe so, but broken bones won't mend that fast."

The porch light came on, and the front door opened.

Porter came out onto the porch. "I thought I heard voices and a truck pull up. Be careful on that ice."

"Who is it, Porter?" Maddy peeked around Porter. "Katie and Will? What's going on?"

Will made it to the porch and lifted Kate off the ice and onto the dry concrete. Will slipped, but Kate held onto him until he caught his balance. Then they hurried into the warm house.

Kate took off her heavy coat, handing it to Porter who took it and hung it in the closet.

Will hugged his parents. "Someone broke into Katie's room again, slashed her wedding dress, and drugged Beebe. The forensic team is checking out the space. I knew she'd be welcome here for the night. I'm going to go back to stay with our guests."

Maddy grabbed Kate in a hug. "I'm so glad you're all right! You are always welcome. Let's get you settled in the guest room again."

"Will …" Kate reached for him.

"It's okay, love. I'll take care of everything." He hugged her and kissed her. "Just get a good night's rest. I'll come get you in the morning after the families leave."

She hugged him. "I love you."

He smiled. "I know."

"Be careful going back."

"I will. Good night." Will smiled and headed out into the wintry weather.

Kate watched from the storm door as Will slid down the driveway to the truck. After he backed out and waved, she waved back and closed the front door.

"What's happening with Beebe?" Maddy grabbed her arm and walked her to the stairs.

"The vet came and took him to the clinic. Whoever it was had injected him with something like a tranquilizer. I don't think I could bear it if he died, Mom." Tears spilled onto her cheeks.

"Try not to worry, Katie. I'm sure you need a rest to deal with it all."

After walking her up the steps, Maddy handed her the overnight bag and closed her in the guest room. She'd stayed there when she first came to Adams to renovate Aunt Katharine's house. It was like coming home. But how could she not worry about what might happen in her house, with guests no less, when she wasn't there? *God, I turn it over to you. I can't do anything to stop the crazy when I'm there, much less when I'm not. Keep Will safe in all the things he's in ... even the secret things.*

When Kate's head sunk into the foam pillow, exhaustion took over.

Chapter 9

After the guests go home …

Taking care on the icy steps, Will entered Katie's house. He breathed a sigh of relief that things seemed quiet and, dare he think, normal. Andy's car and the forensic team van were still parked outside though. Unfortunately, that state of affairs was all too normal.

He climbed the stairs and met Andy at the top. "What's the word?"

"Chaos, that's the word. They incapacitated Beebe, so he wouldn't pay attention to what they were doing. Did he know the intruder? He never barked before being drugged. Careful. Premeditated. Then the dress was slashed to pieces in a fury. And with Katie asleep in the room. It boggles my imagination, Will. I just don't understand. Previously, whoever it was broke the strand of pearls instead of just taking the necklace."

"It doesn't make sense to me either." Will ran his hand through his hair then smoothed it back down. "Do you think Katie is in danger from this maniac?"

The cuckoo sounded nine times.

Andy scratched his nine o'clock shadow. "I hope the forensics will tell us something. Is there anyone who would feel betrayed by you marrying Katie?"

"So, you think it's a woman? You know I never really dated. It was always Katie from when we were ten."

Andy laughed. "Oh, I know. You mooned over Katie for fifteen years, longer than you even knew her. What was the name of the girl who was sleeping in the root cellar last summer?"

"Viola Chastain."

"Oh yeah, the Georgia southern belle." Andy gave a low whistle. "Beautiful but crazy as crackers. Any idea what happened to her after we released her?"

"No, but a stay in a psych ward would have been useful." Will rolled his eyes. He hadn't given her a second thought after she'd been arrested for camping in the root cellar. "I guess it could be her. I don't know how to find her short of checking with her mom."

"You go nowhere near her or her family. If she thinks she's stopping your wedding to Katie and you show up at her house, she might interpret that as courting her." Andy waved his hands. "Let me stand in between to find out if it was her."

"Fine." Will lowered his voice. "Actually, I have a problem I'd like to discuss with you, in private. Preferably when you're not in uniform or in this house or garage."

Andy scrunched his face. "What kind of thing have you gotten into?"

"It's a business contract, but I can't talk about it now. The house could be bugged."

Andy frowned. "You sound paranoid. But you're

only paranoid if someone's *not* out to get you. How 'bout coffee tomorrow afternoon?"

One of the forensic team entered the landing, wearing his zippered protective jumpsuit. "Deputy, I think we've got all the evidence we can get, for now anyway. We'll be ready to head back to the lab once we close up the evidence samples in our kits."

"Good. I'll follow you back to the lab." Andy put his hand on Will's back. "I'll see you tomorrow then for coffee."

Will nodded.

Once Andy and the forensic team left, Will checked the doors and set the security system. Then he stoked the fire in the sitting room, rolled out his sleeping bag, then snuggled into it.

The cuckoo sounded twelve o'clock. He stared into the darkness most of the night, worrying about Katie's safety. She'd been in danger too much of the time that she'd been in Adams. Would being married change that? Who would be threatened by their impending nuptials? What could be done to prevent just anyone from entering the house?

He heard the cuckoo at three o'clock. How was he to do what Demeter wanted without breaking the law?

The next thing he knew, children were running around upstairs, and luggage was being moved.

Oh Lord, help me do what I need to do today.

On Sunday morning, Kate woke in Maddy and

Porter's guest room to bright streaks of sunlight. A look out the window showed a dusting of snow coating the ice underneath. She shivered in her nightgown and headed for the shower. After dressing, she went downstairs to a Maddy breakfast.

"What smells so good, Mom?" Kate came around the kitchen counter to hug Maddy.

"It's Sunday. That's waffle day around here. It's so nice to have you here, Katie." Maddy returned her hug. "It's nice to have time with you. Since you opened the B&B, you've had no time to spend with us here."

Kate shook her head. "It's been so much work. Not the cleaning and cooking, it's the sense of juggling too many balls, so everyone has everything they need while they are there. Layered with the constant threat of something bad happening …"

Maddy nodded. "The stress of the unknown is the worst. Are you putting on your spiritual armor every morning?"

Kate put her elbows on the counter and her chin in her hands. "I try. I really do. Truth is I miss as much as I hit. What's the secret?"

"The secret is wanting that daily connection. The secret to that is knowing you can only get through stuff by having Him by your side. I'm not saying you'll have no problems. You might have more, but He'll be there to help you conquer them." Maddy opened the waffle iron and lifted a steamy waffle onto a plate. She handed it to Kate. "It's like eating breakfast to me. There's never a day that I get up and think, 'I'll skip breakfast today.' I like breakfast, and it's my habit to eat it, every day. So, since Porter doesn't fix it, it's up to me to get up, decide what to fix, and make it happen." She poured more batter into the waffle iron.

"In other words, it's essential."

"Yes. Couldn't step outside my house without breakfast or my God time." Maddy smiled. "It's so good to have girl talk. Could I buy you a devotional to use?"

Kate grinned. "Yes, ma'am. Or just tell me the name of one, and I can buy it myself from Amazon."

"No, let me do this." Maddy took another steaming waffle from the iron and put it on a plate. "Porter left early this morning. Some kind of emergency at the church. I'll drop you by your house after we finish. If all goes well, you and Billy may be able to join us for worship services."

"That would be an answer to prayer: guests who leave on time and without drama." Kate poured syrup on her waffles and then took a bite. "This is wonderful!"

"Only because you didn't have to cook it." Maddy laughed.

"Maybe, but thank you for cooking it for me."

Will was helping the Martins carry and stow luggage in their car when Maddy drove up with Katie. The girls jumped out of their car and ran to greet her like a dear old friend who'd returned. She hugged them both, then found her way to Will. He wrapped her in his arms.

"I'm so glad to see you. I missed you at breakfast." Will kissed her.

She kissed him tenderly and then with urgency. "I missed you too."

"Ooo!" Trevor and Tyler ran down the front walk and fell, sliding just about to the curb. They stood and pointed at Katie and Will. "Katie and Will, sitting in a tree, K-I-S-S-I-N-G!"

Katie blushed a pretty shade of pink. "Well, we are getting married just before Christmas."

The boys laughed and ran off, slipping and sliding, to their own car.

Jordan and Ellen joined Will and Katie. "We have had a relaxing and wonderful holiday weekend. The girls enjoyed the craft and the cookies. The fire in the fireplace and the Christmas tree were homey. I don't think we'll forget our last celebration in the States for three years. Thank you. You were an amazing hostess, even with all the things going on."

Joy and Faith joined them and hugged Katie. "We call this a twin sandwich at our house. We're the bread, but you're the good stuff in the middle."

"I'm glad you had a special time here. Send us a postcard from Germany." Katie hugged them both before they scooted back to their car.

Will and Katie waved as the Martins left.

Soon the Greens stepped down the walkway carrying their one suitcase.

"Why do the folks with more stuff get away before the others?" Will whispered into Katie's ear.

Katie shrugged. Her overnight bag sat on the sidewalk from her night at Chez Bell.

"I'm so glad you're back before we left. Ghastly what happened to your dress and pearls. How is Beebe?" Jenny reached out to Katie and hugged her.

"I haven't heard anything about Beebe yet. I'm sure no news is good news." Katie returned her hug. "Did your boys have a good time?"

"Yes, though they initially thought the cookies and crafts were 'girlie things.'" Jenny emphasized the words with air quotes. "Once they started the activities, they had a great time. Will was a hit with them, too."

Matthias shook Will's hand. "The guys had a great role model in you. A Christian man who loves his girl, protects her, and even cooks breakfast. Thanks for being a real man."

"That's nice. Thanks." Will felt his face warming.

"Next time we need a family weekend away, we'll think of Kate's B&B first." Matthias smiled and herded his boys back to their car.

"Happy wedding, Kate." Jenny waved and climbed into their vehicle.

Soon they also drove away.

"I can't believe it. Guests who actually leave on the day they're supposed to." Katie laughed. "We might be able to go to church."

As Will and Katie headed toward the house, Porter pulled up in his truck and rolled down the window.

"No services today. The church was vandalized. It's a mess. Police are there now."

Chapter 10

Vandalized church …

"We could have had services." Kate walked with Will from the parking lot into the church. "Plenty of church members turned out to view the destruction to the church."

Will nodded. When it was their turn to see the problem, they stepped up to the entry doors.

Red paint spelled out the vandal's message, "Kate is Bell Witch devil servant."

"Are we back to that? I thought that rumor was laid to rest last summer." Kate groaned. "It's too much to take in. I can't even go back to my own bedroom with the police tape up."

Sarah and her husband Paul came into the vestibule to view the damage behind Kate and Will. "Oh, Katie, not again!"

"And someone has accessed my bedroom two days in a row. Beebe is at the vet clinic, having been drugged by the intruder. My pearl necklace is broken, and my wedding dress has been slashed to ribbons."

"I am so sorry." Sarah hugged her. "Have you ever

met my sister Jane?”

A mousy, brown-haired girl came from behind her. "Hello."

"Hi, Jane. I hear you work at the bakery with Sarah." Kate smiled.

"I help with the bread. Sarah lets me help in the shop too." She smiled a crooked grin. "Hello, Billy. You're my friend."

Will hugged her. "That's right, Jane."

Jane's face lit up at his touch. "You said I your special friend."

"Absolutely. Always." Will gave her a wide smile.

Jane blushed and hid her mouth behind her hand. "You always nice to me. Why you marry Kate?"

"Katie has been my best friend for a long time, almost as long as we've been alive. We want to live together for the rest of our lives." Will held her hand as he spoke to her. "We can still be friends, though."

A cloud seemed to cross over her eyes. Tears formed. "Oh, not your special friend no more because Kate is."

Sarah spoke up. "Jane is also working part-time at the vet clinic. She helps with the dogs and cats."

An alarm went off in Kate's mind. *Is Jane jealous of my relationship with Will?*

Jane leaned toward Kate. "I saw Beebe this morning when I fed dogs. He still sleeping."

Kate took Jane's other hand. "Take good care of Beebe for me when you're there."

"I always do." She pulled her hand from Kate's. "Beebe's a good dog."

The crowd in the foyer grew. The pastor called out, "If you've seen the damage, could you step outside so others can come in.”

Will pulled his hand from Jane's. “I need to go home now. I'll see you later.”

Jane nodded. “Later. Promise?”

“Of course.” Will patted her shoulder. “See you later, Alligator.”

“In a while, Crocodile.” Jane laughed at their silly exchange. “I look for you.”

Will nodded and led Kate down the heavily salted steps. He opened the passenger door for Kate to step into his beat-up red truck. After closing her door, Will came around to the driver's side and climbed in.

Kate touched his arm. “Do you think Jane is jealous of me marrying you?”

“Jane? Jealous?” Will squinted as he thought. “No, she's simple but not stupid. She knows she and I are not in love. We're just friends.”

“Like you and Viola Chastain?” Kate removed her hand.

Will started the truck and put it in gear. He glanced over at Katie. She'd gone silent over Jane. Did she really think Jane could get to the B&B on her own in a storm twice in one weekend, inject Beebe with anything, or destroy the pearl necklace and the wedding dress? All of it was ludicrous, too unlikely to be believed. But someone had done all of that.

“If not Jane or Viola, who would have done these things?”

Katie's voice was quiet. He sorta wished she'd

scream at him. He honestly had no idea who was tormenting his fiancee. Demeter and his crew wouldn't care to slice up a wedding dress or spill a pearl necklace. They would have held her at knifepoint or pulled a gun on her or Beebe.

"I don't know who could have done these things." Will took care on the icy roads. The sun was melting the ice, but some spots were still treacherous. "Let's go back to the house. I have a feeling the sheriff's men will want to talk to us – again."

Katie put her hand over her face. "I'm so embarrassed about all the attention I've received in Adams, for all the wrong reasons. What do we have to do? Run away to someplace no one knows us?"

Will pulled the note he'd found in her room. "What's this note about?"

"Where did you find it?" Katie held up the note that read 'DON'T MARRY WILL BELL'.

"I found it on your bed when we were picking up pearls."

"I didn't see it."

Will pulled up in front of the house. "But you don't look surprised."

"No. This warning is the second time I've heard this. Young Murray MacGowan told me the Bell Witch said I shouldn't marry into the Bell family." Katie twisted her ring around her finger. "I don't believe in the Bell Witch, but I do believe in evil people who are not above using superstition to scare others."

"I would have liked to have known about this sooner." Will hopped out of the cab and raced around the truck, sliding in some spots, to open Katie's door. "Be careful of the ice."

Will and Katie walked and slid up to the house. The front door stood open. When Katie looked at him, he shook his head.

They stepped into the foyer. Katie checked the reception desk for anything out of order. Finding nothing amiss, Will and Katie moved together to check out the first floor: sitting room, living room, dining room, and kitchen. Nothing.

Will whispered to Katie. "Stay here. I'll check upstairs."

Will took the steps to the second floor and ran across the hallway to Katie's bedroom. When he looked in over the police tape, he saw her wedding shoes cut in pieces and strewn all over her bedroom. It was obvious to him. Someone didn't want them to marry, Bell Witch or not. The results were the same.

Katie's perfume snuck up on him.

Will turned and clasped her in his arms. "Don't look." He turned Katie away from the chaos in her room.

She tried to look into the room, but Will held her tight. "Did they come back? What did they do now? The shoes were the only things left for the wedding."

"Let's go downstairs and make coffee. Any of those croissants left from Sarah's Bakery?"

Katie crumpled in his arms. "I have no wedding clothing left?" She sobbed on his shoulder.

Will picked Katie up and carried her down the stairs to the kitchen table. Then he released her into the comfort of a chair.

"I don't understand. Why would someone go to so much effort?" She wiped her face with a napkin. "I spent money getting that dress restored. It took forever to find the right shoes. My pearls …”

“Don’t think on it, sweetheart. Try not to think about it. You can wear whatever you like to our wedding.” Will started the coffeemaker. The whirring sound of the grinder released the aroma of coffee. “It’ll be ready soon. Two beautiful croissants for us.” He put them on plates and placed one in front of Katie.

She attempted a smile, but it never made it to her eyes.

Will kneeled beside her. “I’m so sorry all this happened. We could elope instead.”

“No, most emphatically no. I don’t plan to marry more than one time, so I want it to be memorable.” A spark shone in her eyes. “No one will keep me from marrying you, especially after you bundled all that mistletoe.”

Steam escaped the coffeemaker, accentuating her remark and signaling the end of the brewing cycle. A loud boom indicated that something had fallen upstairs.

“We didn’t check the other bedrooms.” Katie shrank in her chair. “We’re not safe.”

Will swore under his breath. He handed Katie his phone. “Call Andy now.” Then he headed toward the sound.

Chapter 11

More to come …

Will climbed the stairs as quietly as he could, listening for the next noise to determine the whereabouts of the intrusion. Katie's room was closed off with yellow police tape intact. He crept down the hall until he heard a sound in bedroom number three.

Standing beside the open door, Will listened. Katie always left the doors to the rooms open after the guests left to air them out. She also checked for left-behind items then. Since they'd gone to church after the families left, the doors were open, but she hadn't gone through the rooms yet.

When he heard a sound again, Will jumped into the room, hoping to surprise the intruder.

The window was open, and the cold winter breeze blew the curtains, making a clacking sound with the valance rings on the rod. The room appeared empty. He searched until he heard it again. He approached the window with caution.

On closer inspection, the window wasn't open, it was broken. A brick lay on the floor below it. A note was wrapped around it. A sinking feeling left no doubt what it would say.

"What did you find?" Katie's question made Will jump. "Anything?"

Will picked up the brick and showed it to Katie. "Any thoughts about what this note says?"

"It's Sunday. There shouldn't be mail today." Katie laughed at her own joke. "The window's broken then as well."

"It is. I don't guess they can get fingerprints from a brick. Did you get hold of Andy?"

"He's on his way … again." Katie sat on the edge of the bed. "This is ridiculous."

The security chime on the front door dinged.

Will moved to the top of the stairs and hollered down. "We're in bedroom three."

Andy climbed the stairs. He had no vigor in his step. When he reached the landing, he sighed. "What's going on now?"

"You okay?" Will gave him a bro hug. "You're looking tired, friend."

"Short night. Many places to be. Mayhem on every hand." Andy turned toward Katie. "How are you?"

"Except for the brick through my window and all my wedding finery destroyed, I'm just peachy." Katie flashed a wry smile. "Someone cut up my shoes while we were at church."

"Then there's this." Will handed the brick to Andy. "There's also a note."

"It's possible to get fingerprints from the note, but probably not from the brick." Andy pulled a large evidence bag from his pocket and opened it. He placed the brick inside. Slipping on neoprene gloves, Andy released the string around the note and took it out of the bag. "Let's see what your Sunday morning delivery guy has to say."

Andy opened the folded paper and laid it on the bed. "DON'T MARRY WILL BELL!" it read in red block letters.

Will pulled the note from Katie's bedroom out of his pocket and lay it beside the new note. "Looks like the same person wrote both."

"Where'd this one come from?" Andy's eyebrows arched and joined together.

Will shook his head. "In Katie's room after the pearls were spilled."

Andy examined them side by side. "Same printer. Who wants you out of the picture, Will?" He marked the bags.

He shrugged and wrapped an arm around Katie.

Andy shivered. "You better board up that window. The breeze is wintry. I'll take both notes into forensics." He pulled out a smaller bag and put both notes in it. "I love you guys, but seriously, could we quit meeting like this?"

Kate went back down the familiar stairs. *Was it worth the trouble?* The cooking, baking, brewing? Having strangers in the house that break things, some irreplaceable? She sighed as she stepped onto the main floor. When she reached the dining room, she heard sounds beyond the dining room. She had a flashback to the raccoon in her kitchen. Her heartbeat revved up.

Who or what was in there?

As she reached the door, Sarah approached her from inside the kitchen. "Hi, Katie. The door was unlocked, so I went ahead and brought your order in. It's on the table. Is something wrong?"

"What isn't wrong?" Will appeared behind Kate, startling her. "You've been over to the church to see the latest vandalism. Did you hear about Katie's wedding dress? Pearls? Shoes?"

Sarah stepped back from him. "Whoa! Why the twenty questions? All I did was bring you baked goods."

Katie placed a hand on Will's arm. "Someone has been getting into the house. They broke my pearl necklace and took a knife to my dress and shoes. They also drugged Beebe, and he's still at the vet's. As you know, someone vandalized the church as well."

Will added, "And someone just threw a brick through an upstairs window."

"The door was open when I got here." Sarah set the tray down beside her. "You don't think I would do anything to hurt you, do you? I thought we were friends."

"Will's just on edge." Kate stroked his arm, hoping he'd turn back into his usual, affable self.

"Paul's waiting in the truck. I just thought I'd bring your order while we were nearby." Sarah picked up the tray. "I hope things level out. What will you do about your dress?"

Kate shrugged. "Do you have time to go shopping this week? Maybe I can find something I can afford."

"Wedding dress shopping?" Sarah gave a squeal. "I'd love to do that. Tell me when."

"Check your calendar and text me when you're available." Kate smiled.

"Knock, knock!" A male voice called out from the front door. "Sarah?"

"It's Paul. I better go." Sarah scurried to the foyer.

By then, Paul was in the house. "What are you doing? I thought this would be fast."

Will was right behind her and stuck out his hand to greet him. "Hey, Paul."

He grabbed his hand and pumped it. "Sorry about all the trouble you're having. Say, we're headed back to Springfield to get lunch. We dropped Jane by the vet clinic for afternoon duty. Want to come with us?"

Kate nodded. "Absolutely. Where?"

Will looked to Kate. "We need to secure the house first. Andy's still upstairs making another police report. We could meet you somewhere in a bit."

"Sounds great." Sarah hugged Kate. "Text me when you're available, and I'll text you the place."

Andy came down the stairs as Sarah and Paul were leaving. "Your house is like Grand Central Station. People are always coming and going."

Kate nodded. "Therein lies the rub."

Andy pointed to Will. "Are we still meeting this afternoon?"

"That would be great. Remember not in uniform." Will held his finger to his lips.

"Call me when you get back from lunch." Andy shook his head. "I'm eager to hear about your secret project. Are you in trouble?"

"Afraid so."

Chapter 12

The secret, dangerous project …

Will pulled up in front of Joelton Hardware, Feed, & Farmacy. Food, hardware, and live music. *What a concept! Dad would never go for it in his hardware store in the middle of Adams, but it could be fun once in a while.* Hopefully Demeter and his biker gang wouldn't frequent it.

He walked in, looking for Andy. A raised hand caught his attention.

Andy sat at an out-of-the-way table. He fit right in with his plaid flannel shirt and jeans. Hopefully no one would notice him as a member of the Robertson County Sheriff Office.

Will made his way to the table. Before sitting down, he removed his coat and draped it on the back of his chair. A waitress was at his elbow as soon as he settled into his place.

"Can I get you something to drink, guys?"

Andy handed her the menu. "Just coffee."

Will nodded. "Same."

She took the menus. "Pie? We've got a fresh apple

pie."

Will sighed. "Bring me a piece."

Andy laughed. "Me too."

She cracked her gum. "I'll be right back."

Andy drummed on the table. "Before we talk about your secret project, can we talk about the wedding?"

"What do you need to know?"

Andy leaned in. "What are we wearing? Tuxes? Matching suits?"

Will shrugged. "I don't really know. Now that Katie's dress is destroyed, it may be different. Sarah and Katie are planning a shopping trip for this week. I should know more after that."

Andy's face showed distress. "Dude, literally two weeks away."

"I'll ask what Katie wants." Will shook his head. "I don't know. The wedding is important, but it's on the back burner compared to all the other stuff happening."

The waitress appeared with cups of coffee and plates of pie. "Let me know if y'all need anything else."

Both of them nodded.

"So, tell me what's going on with you." Andy sipped the coffee before picking up his fork. "You talk; I'll enjoy the pie."

Will took a sip of coffee. "The guy I worked for in Nashville offered me the opportunity to do a job, off-the-books, for $25,000. The trick was that if I opened the document, I accepted the job."

"Sounds sketchy. You should know better than that." Andy scooped up a bite of pie.

"You're right. I should, and I do, but I did." Will twirled his fork in the whipped cream on the pie. "The document had some kind of geo-tag that sent my information to a guy named Demeter."

Andy sputtered and choked a bit on his pie. "He's a bad dude to be involved with."

Will wiped his hand across his forehead. "We had a surprise meeting in my garage/office including his two henchmen Friday night. Basically, what I'm doing is exactly what Demeter warned me not to do."

"What's the job?" Andy put down his fork and gave Will his full attention.

"The gang has a delivery coming around Christmas, and they need a bunker to store whatever it is. They own a piece of land where they plan to sink a shipping container. My job is to design the interior air transfer system."

Andy frowned. "Any idea what the shipment is going to be?"

Will shook his head. "They want the design now. I can do it, but I don't think I should. I don't want to put Katie in any more peril than she already is."

"I can see why the wedding is on the back burner. Where is the land? Do they have the container?"

Will placed his face in his hands. "I don't know how much to tell you. I'm not supposed to tell you anything." Will pulled a folded piece of paper from his shirt pocket. "Here are the particulars. I know the container is on-site waiting for my ventilation system to be installed."

Andy opened the page. "Have you completed the system?"

"I'm almost done. I gave into financial insecurity." Will shook his head. "I should never have opened the document. The money tempted me. I gave in to my fear."

Andy's eyebrows joined. "Is the B&B not making money? You seem to have a full house most weekends."

"Katie is the hostess with the mostest. She wants our guests to have everything they need and most of what they want. Unfortunately, everything costs money. What we're charging doesn't cover all the things Katie wants to provide. Hence my giving into temptation." Will twisted his mouth. "Am I abetting a crime?"

Andy shook his head. "No, telling me about it is like you're a confidential informant. I'll get the TBI involved. The crime is most likely across state borders, so the FBI could have jurisdiction. Let me work this. Do what you've been ordered to do. I'll keep your name out of any records or warrants."

"Is the pie not good?" The waitress startled both men.

Andy recovered first. "It's very good. We just are having some serious conversation today."

She held her hands up. "Sorry to bother you. I'll leave you alone. Just holler if I can help."

Will sucked in a breath. "Do you think Demeter's gang knows her? What if this was a bad idea? What if she tells him we were here?"

Andy shook his head. "I'm sure it's okay, and I know you needed to let me know what's happening. They could be the ones terrorizing Katie. Regardless, we need to stop Demeter and his gang. One more thing."

Will drew closer to him. "What?"

"Eat your pie." Andy laughed and forked a piece into his mouth.

Kate walked from Sarah's car to her own front door. She waved to Paul and Sarah. They had brought her home since Will had that meeting with Andy, telling him things he was afraid to tell her. Unfortunately, she was a little afraid to enter the house or be in there alone. Beebe wasn't even there to be with her. *Nothing to be done about it. Will had to take care of his business, just as I have to take care of mine.*

The afternoon sun was already beginning to set. She unlocked the front door and turned off the alarm system. Then she closed the door and threw the deadbolt in place. When she turned around, Kate saw the beautiful tree. Plugging in the lights made it even better. It made her smile, that and the profusion of mistletoe that Will had managed to hang all over the place. She turned on the Christmas music on the intercom, soothingly soft. She kicked shoes off and plopped down with her Christmas novel, pulling her legs up under her. She opened to the red ribbon bookmark. She'd read until Will arrived home.

Kate guessed that some would say they were living together, and in some ways it was true. But they were not sleeping together in any imaginable way. Sometimes he slept in the living room in a sleeping bag. Most times he slept in the garage on a convertible sofa. He only began sleeping on the premises after having strangers in the house became frightening, and strange things began happening.

She wondered where she was sleeping tonight. Probably back at Mom and Dad Bell's again. Kate loved Will's parents, but she didn't want them to grow tired of her presence and the constant drama going on at her B&B.

Kate checked her phone for the time or for a text from Will. Four o'clock. The sun was near to setting. *Hope he's okay.* She turned on the lamp to offset the shadows. She finally delved into the book.

It was fully dark when Kate looked up from her read. Except for her lamp and the Christmas tree, the house was dark. She checked the time again. Five o'clock. *Where was Will?* She put the red ribbon in her book.

Then she heard a noise in the kitchen. A scratching at the door, a turning of the lock. Will hadn't texted, so it shouldn't be him. *Who is at the back door with a key?*

Chapter 13

The mysterious visitor …

Kate heard another sound at the kitchen door. She put down her book then picked up the poker from the fireplace. She took a deep breath and headed for the kitchen. All of her nerves were on fire, and she tightened her grip. The poker shook as she moved.

Kate crept through the dark house to the kitchen. She left the lights off, thinking that might be to her advantage as she peeked out the window. Someone – she couldn't tell who – stood on the stoop, rifling through his or her pockets. She held the poker up as high as she could with one hand. Her heart thudded in her chest. She flipped on the porch light and ripped open the door.

"Katie! What are you doing?" The figure cried out and held his arm over his face.

"Will! Why are you sneaking in the kitchen door? Don't you have your keys?"

Will grabbed her arm with the poker and lowered it. "Are you trying to kill me?" He took the poker and leaned it in a corner.

"Of course not. I was prepared to rain terror on a stranger trying to break into the house." Kate stepped back, so Will could enter the kitchen. "Don't scare me like that again. Call me when you're on your way home."

Will wrapped his arms around her. "Home. I like the sound of that."

"You have to live long enough to get to the wedding, sweetheart." Kate crossed her arms.

Will hugged her closer. "Darling, question one, where are you sleeping tonight?"

"Don't know. I can make up one of the other rooms until the police tape comes down in mine."

"The slush is refreezing in the streets. It's going to be more treacherous driving the later it gets. Question two, where do you want me to sleep?" Will raised his eyebrows. "I can sleep in the garage, though it is really cold despite the mini-split."

"Don't know. You could sleep in one of the other bedrooms. That way you'll be close when an intruder breaks in."

Will scrunched his eyebrows together. "When an intruder breaks in? Don't you mean 'if'?"

"At this point, 'when' is the appropriate word. We have never been able to keep anyone out who wanted to get into the house." Kate relocked the kitchen door.

Will shrugged. "You're right. Let's go into the living room by the fire."

They settled on the burgundy velvet settee. After Will sat down, Kate sat next to him and leaned back against his chest. His heartbeat soothed her, and the twinge in her chest uncoiled. He put his arms around her, making her feel safe from the rest of the world. The fire was only coals, but it still put out comfortable heat into the room.

She took a deep breath. "Can you tell me what you told Andy about the secret contract? After all, I am your partner in business and in life. What comes to you also comes to me."

Will was silent for a few moments. Kate wondered if he'd fallen asleep. The coals in the fireplace popped.

"I only want you to be safe. The less you know, the safer you'll be." He hugged her tighter. "I couldn't bear to lose you again."

"I feel those exact things about you. Whatever affects you also affects me. Forever, sweetheart. If you're in trouble, I want – no need – to know how to help you." Kate squeezed his arms around her. "How can I avoid danger if I don't know where it's coming from?"

Will sighed. "You're right, but you're already in danger from someone who doesn't want us to marry. That's more than enough for me to worry about."

"What's that saying? 'A problem shared is a problem halved.' We're hopefully going to be married for a long time. Sharing our worries is Marriage 101." She raised his hand to her lips and kissed his palm.

After a deep exhale, Will began the woeful tale. "The contract pays $25,000. I had to decide to take the contract, sight unseen. I thought we needed the money because the B&B isn't making any money. In fact, we're losing money every weekend. It's not sustainable."

Her breath caught in her chest. "You never told me, but I figured that was true when you fussed about the beef stew."

"Anyway, I thought we needed the money. Turns out when I opened the file, it sent my name and location back to the head honcho of a biker gang who is known as Demeter. According to Andy, they're well-known to the constabulary." Will paused. "Are you sure you want to know more about this?"

"Every detail." Even though her heart seemed to cramp in her chest. She flashed back to the heart attack she'd had in the ambulance in July. She'd been frightened by her ex-boyfriend Brian, leading to a fall through the attic trapdoor into the saferoom one floor below. The fractures in her back ached much of the time, and her heart damage caused her pain in difficult situations. The back and heart docs had not released her yet. Still, this was her business, not just Will's. "Go on."

"All right. They have some kind of merchandise coming in around Christmas. I didn't ask what. They plan to stash it in an underground bunker made from a shipping container. They want the bunker to be habitable in case they need to hide in it. It needs an access from the ground above it. Then, in short, it needs an air-handling system to provide oxygen to the space underground."

Kate interrupted him. "So they don't die underground. Is that hard?"

"No. But without the building permits, inspections, et cetera, it's illegal. They have the land and the shipping container. I need to purchase and install the air-handling system."

When he paused, Kate straightened up and looked at Will. "Can that all be done by Christmas? That's less than three weeks. The wedding is before Christmas."

"In short, not really. Just ordering the exchange unit will be hard." Will pulled her back to him. "That's why I needed to get Andy involved despite the threats about telling anyone."

"At least I know how to pray. Could we pray together now?"

"I'd like nothing more than that right now." Will began a prayer for wisdom and for God to keep Katie and himself safe from harm.

She startled awake. In her sleepy haze, Kate counted the cuckoos, coming up with eleven. Eleven! She was still in Will's arms. He was snoring softly. Then she heard the sound that had awakened her. Footsteps on the creaky stairs. Will was the only other person who was supposed to be in the house.

"Will." She shook him and whispered. "Someone else is in the house with us. They're on the stairs."

He kept his eyes closed. "Are you sure it's not just settling sounds since it's so cold tonight?"

"I don't know what it is, but that's the point. We're the only ones here. Even Beebe is at the vet's."

That remark seemed to rouse him. "How did they get in without us knowing it?"

"That's a great question. What are we going to do about it?" Kate's adrenaline was pumping.

"I'll call Andy first. Then we're going to slip out of the house to the garage. Put on your boots and grab your coat and purse." Will opened his phone and called Andy. "Hey, Andy. We need someone to come now, silently. There's an intruder in the house."

Kate slipped on her boots and coat. After grabbing her purse, she headed to the kitchen. The snow was still coming down and under the snow was ice. Early December in Tennessee was not snow weather. What were January and February going to look like?

Will entered the kitchen. "What are you still doing here? Go to the garage."

"I don't have keys to your new locks, for one thing."

He sighed. "I have a set for you in my desk. Come on." He opened the kitchen door and sent her out into the snow. "Be careful on the steps, sweetheart."

They slipped and slid all the way to the garage. Will pulled out his keys and opened the locks he'd installed. They entered, then Will refastened all the locks. It wasn't long until the flashing lights from Andy's cruiser played across the garage.

Chapter 14

Turning personal …

Will opened the garage door after removing the padlock he'd affixed that weekend after Demeter's visit. Andy slipped in, and Will closed the door back.

Andy and Katie watched Will affix the padlock back once again.

Andy furrowed his brow. "Dude, a padlock on your door that can only be opened with a remote?"

"I don't need Demeter in my office again." Will moved to the door to the garden and began unlocking the multiple locks he'd installed there.

"Um, this guy really shook you up, didn't he?" Andy placed a hand on his shoulder.

"He wasn't playing." Will disengaged the last lock and opened the door. "Katie, why don't you stay here while …"

"I know you're not going to say 'while the real men keep you safe in the locked garage.' If that's what you're thinking, I'd advise you to keep it unsaid. My house, my problem, too." Katie crossed her arms.

Andy chuckled. "Absolutely, come with us."

Will struggled with Katie's independence in serious situations. She was no weak, fragile creature, even though at times she was overwhelmed. He still wanted to keep her safe. "Yes, my love. At least stay between us."

"I can do that. If we don't hurry, we won't catch whoever it is in the act."

Will turned back to lock the door.

"Will, come on. No one is going into your office at midnight on Sunday evening or Monday morning." Katie waved her hand at him to hurry.

"In case you've forgotten what we're doing, someone thought it was a good time to break into the house." Will crossed his arms in defiance. "I'm just trying to keep us safe."

"Both of you need to hush while we make entry into the house. Is this door bolted as well?" Andy reached for the kitchen door, avoiding the icy patches on the steps.

"No. It's not even locked." Katie huffed.

Will reached out to her and steadied her on the icy steps. "Please be careful. I don't want our wedding in a hospital."

"Ditto to you, Sweetheart."

She was miffed. He could tell. If he didn't love her, he wouldn't be so protective of her.

The three 'musketeers' stepped into the house as quietly as three people could. Sounds still came from upstairs.

Katie whispered to them. "What if I go up through the hidden passageways? I might be able to surprise whoever it is while you cover the door."

Will was shaking his head when Andy answered.

"Sounds like a plan."

"Be careful, Katie." Will grabbed her hand as she opened the butler's pantry. "I love you."

"I know. I'll be fine. Promise." With that, she disappeared into the bowels of the house.

When Will turned back to Andy, he was laughing at them. "You two crack me up. She's not the fair damsel you'd like to control."

"Don't I know it. Let's get moving. I don't want her in that room alone with whatever crazy person is up there." Will shoved Andy.

"Okay. Let's go."

Andy and Will tiptoed up the stairs as fast as possible without making any sound. Will had never noticed how creaky the steps were in a quiet house. Maybe because mayhem reigned most of the time.

They crept toward the open bedroom door and peeked in. The police tape had been ripped down and thrown into the hallway. The intruder wore black sweats with a hood drawn up over his head. He was emptying drawers and strewing things across the room. Everyone noticed when Katie opened the wall because she was using a flashlight.

Alerted to her presence, the intruder headed for the door where Will and Andy waited.

"Gotcha!" yelled Andy.

Will flipped on the hall light while Andy pulled the hoodie down from his head. Katie gasped at the destruction in her room and at the revelation of the perpetrator.

"Brian! What are you doing here?" Katie was floored to see her ex-boyfriend standing amid the ruin of her bedroom.

The man smiled an unsavory leer. "If you won't marry me, you're not marrying anyone else."

Will formed a fist and punched him. With a bleeding nose, Brian went down.

"Why did you do that?" Katie grabbed a towel from the floor and rushed over to the unconscious, bleeding man.

As he came to, Andy pulled him up from the floor and slapped handcuffs on him.

"Brian, you are under arrest for breaking and entering, mischief, and trespass."

"What about Will over there? He broke my nose!" Brian shrieked.

"He was subduing you while in the act of fleeing the scene. A perfectly legal act." Andy grinned. "And he'd better not do it again."

While the men jabbered at each other, Kate looked around her bedroom, at least what was left of it. This destruction was different that the first three. Those break-ins only targeted her wedding finery, such as it was. Brian's attack on her space was frenzied, and nothing was spared from his tantrum. Everything was on the floor. Most of it had been torn, trashed, or disheveled. Most she may as well throw away.

Kate reached down and grabbed a pair of jeans and a T-shirt. She found a hanger to hang them on. She picked up a pair of shoes and put them back on the floor of the closet. Truthfully, she didn't have a lot of personal belongings. Her business attire from her job on

Music Row still hung in the back of the closet, but it was not appropriate for running a bed and breakfast. Will didn't have to tell her they weren't making any money. If they were, she'd have gone shopping for clothes. As it was, she was wearing clothes she'd worn to class in college.

"Don't pick up in there!" Andy's reminder that forensics would be out sometime today, since it was after midnight, to take pictures of the disaster that was her room and belongings.

She grabbed the jeans, T-shirt, and the sneakers. Then she took her mom's Bible and snagged a nightgown from the floor and carried them out. "Just something to wear tomorrow." She hoped there would be underwear in the dryer downstairs. Otherwise, she'd be on another reconnaissance mission in the morning.

"Okay if I go to bed in another room?" Kate tried to keep the sarcasm out of her tone. "I'm just exhausted, guys."

Will joined her in the hall. "What can I do to help?"

"A key for bedroom number three, a set of sheets, and some towels." She entered the bedroom and moved the dirty linen into the hall.

When Will arrived with fresh linen, he helped her make the bed. "Are you okay?"

"I wouldn't say that at this point. Hopefully I will be, though. I'm just exhausted, mentally as well as physically."

Will wrapped his arms around her. "I'm so sorry all this is happening around us. Maybe once we're married, your jilted boyfriends will understand that there's no hope." He grinned and lifted her chin with his index finger. Then he kissed her. "Try to sleep."

Kate nodded. "Good night, my love." She gently shoved him out of the room, undressed, and climbed into the freshly made bed. Sleep, however, was elusive.

She listened to Will and Andy talk to Brian. He vigorously denied any responsibility for the previous destruction in her room. He shouted that he still loved her. And that's why he'd torn up everything she owned? That's not love. Finally, she heard Will, Andy, and Brian exit through the kitchen.

In a few minutes, she heard Will return and set the alarm system.

Will crept up the stairs, and the hallway lights went out. He settled in the room across the hall. Nothing would have calmed her more than him snuggled in the bed with her, but that was still two weeks away. If they made it that long.

Chapter 15

In the light of day …

Kate awakened to a tapping on her door. When she opened her eyes, the sun streaming in the windows around the curtains blinded her. Snow plus sunshine. What time was it anyway?

"Who's there?" She attempted to escape the tangled bed linens. Silly, it had to be Will.

"A cup of coffee and your fiancé." Will's voice, of course.

A glance at her phone told her it was nine o'clock. Kate couldn't remember the last time she'd slept that late. "I don't have my robe."

"I do. Forensics officers were here, took pictures, and released your bedroom from being a crime scene." He always knew what she was thinking.

"Okay, hand it to me when I crack open the door."

"The coffee or the robe?"

Kate smiled. She loved him more than she could imagine loving anyone else. "The robe. Then I'll join you for coffee."

She hid behind the door and opened it. Will's arm

appeared with her robe in his hand. He waved the robe around until she caught it. When he withdrew his arm, Kate slammed the door shut.

Will's deep laugh made her smile. "I won't need a ring on that hand if you are any faster with that door."

"Oh, no!" One of those drawers that Brian had dumped on the floor had held Will's wedding ring. "I'll be a few minutes. I need to find something from one of the dumped drawers."

"Okay. Should I be concerned?"

"Not yet. Only if I can't find it should you worry."

"I'll keep the coffee warm. But I can't guarantee a croissant if you take too long." He laughed an evil sounding laugh. Then he affected a French accent, "The croissants are all mine."

After Kate slipped on her robe, she hurried to the staircase and called down. "You promised coffee and croissants!" She giggled. Life with Will would never be dull.

She flipped the lights on in her bedroom and found the drawer that had held the ring. She dug around in the mess, putting things back into the drawer. She finished without finding it. *It's a small box. Maybe it bounced.* She poked around, picking up and folding things, and replacing drawers in her bureau. Still no ring.

"Hey, what's going on? We can clean up this mess after breakfast." Will's deep voice rumbled through her.

"Your ring is missing. It was in this drawer! Now I can't find it!" Her voice rose as she became more concerned. "Did Brian take it or was it the person who destroyed my pearls, dress, and shoes?"

Will's eyebrows furrowed. "I'll give Andy a call. They probably still have Brian in custody."

Kate nodded and continued sorting through her things. She had no idea when it had gone missing. She'd been kept from her room ever since the dress had been slashed to pieces. For all she knew, it had gone missing on the day that the strand of pearls had been broken. The longer she looked, the more desperate she felt. Her heart pounded. The ring had been purchased and engraved specifically for Will. It took time – time they no longer had before the wedding.

What did she have left for the wedding? Only herself and Will. And God. Tears formed. Why did someone want to stop their wedding?

Will pulled out his phone and dialed Andy.

He answered on the first ring. "What's up now, Will? People will begin to talk about how often we chat and meet up."

"Something precious is missing from Katie's room. Any chance you took it from Brian last night when you took him into custody?" Will walked out onto the front porch. "It's my wedding ring."

"Oh, that's painful, especially after her dress, shoes, and pearls have been decimated. I will check his personals and the back of the cruiser. If he had it, he could have discarded it on the way to the car. Check the yard."

"Thanks. I'll take a look."

Will walked out onto the slick front lawn. He followed the footprints across the yard to the curb. He slipped a few times but caught himself. He bent to examine several holes in the ice. Nothing. If it wasn't Brian, who was focused on disrupting the wedding?

When he entered the house again, Katie met him at the door.

"What did Andy say?" She took his arm and walked with him toward the kitchen.

"He didn't have anything when he was taken into custody. I just searched the ice field that is in the front yard. I didn't find it there."

Katie slunk into a kitchen chair. "So, should we just give up? On the house, on the wedding, on the businesses?"

Will crouched beside her. "No. God would not want us to just give up. If it's worth fighting for, it's what we should do. I love you. No matter what. I want to marry you and spend my life with you. Will it be easy? Maybe not. Are you ready to give up on us?"

Katie sighed. "No. Of course not. But who is it who wants me to give up?"

Will shrugged. "The weather is calling for warm sunshine. We can check the yard again once the ice melts. Let me pour you some coffee, then I can help you clear away the mess in your room."

"It's Monday. I need to wash the sheets and towels and clean the rooms." Katie sweetened and creamed her coffee. Then she took a sip.

"Maybe you should take today off. What are our guests doing this coming weekend?"

She grabbed a brochure from the table. "Wrapping packages, singing Christmas carols, making your mom's crafty ornaments again. The brochure says wassailing. We'll see about that."

Will nodded. "We need a wrapping station with Christmas paper, ribbon and bows, tape, gift cards, and red pens and markers. I'll go buy stuff for it today after I check out the project worksite."

"Where is the work site?"

Will shrugged. "All I have are GPS coordinates to put into my phone. What else is happening?"

"I have Christmas movies listed on the next weekend. Maybe we should watch one on Friday night." Katie tapped her finger on the table. "I could mix up more cookie dough as an alternative if we run out of things to do."

"Or here's a thought, they could unwind in the sitting room or play the piano or read a Christmas-y book. Do we have children as guests again this weekend?" Will took the croissants from the warm oven and placed the stoneware on the trivet. "I know you want to help direct our guests' activities, but perhaps they just want to chill without so much structure. Provide the options, then step back and let them be as busy as they want to be."

He sat beside her. "You need to focus on being the bride at our wedding. Go shopping for a new dress and shoes. Mom's getting the pearls restrung. What other arrangements do we need to make?"

"Sarah's making our cake. Pastor Bob is officiating. Your dad is walking me to the altar. Donna and Kathy are doing the flowers. I'd like some poinsettias for the house."

Will arched an eyebrow. "Do we need more mistletoe? We have more in the cellar."

"I guess you could offer mistletoe wrapping sessions to the guys." She chuckled.

"Or we could hook up a TV down there to watch football." He made his eyebrows dance.

Katie gave him a slant-eyed look.

"It's a thought." Will grinned. "The ladies can have a Christmas tea." He picked up his mug with an outstretched pinkie.

"I'd need to make tea cakes and cucumber sandwiches." Katie cocked her head to the side.

"What's wrong with Christmas cookies and hot tea? Don't make more work or expense. Just set the table and let the ladies talk and drink tea." Will took her hand. "You will burn out before Christmas if you don't stop creating more work for yourself."

She nodded. "I see what you're saying. Shouldn't I be around though?"

Will shook his head. "You don't have to be. You're setting the opportunities to enjoy these things. Didn't I see a Christmas tea pot and fancy teacups?"

Katie perked up. "Yes, and little plates to match. They were Aunt Katharine's. We used to have a real tea party for what we called Christmas in July. I'd forgotten that. They're still in the built-in corner china cabinet."

"There you go, Sweetheart. Christmas tea." Will finished a croissant. "I need to get going to the project site. Will you be okay alone until dinner today?"

"Of course. I'll lock up and set the alarm system while I shower and dress. Then I'll start the laundry and go out to look at dresses. Sarah wanted to come with me, so I'll check with her."

Will stood and kissed her. "I'll see you soon. Be careful on the icy roads."

Chapter 16

Working for a solution ….

Will stayed until Sarah arrived for their shopping trip. He waved to Katie and Sarah as they pulled away from the curb in Sarah's car. Even though Katie had a new car after replacing the blue one, she couldn't forget seeing Tara, dead, in her vehicle in the garage. He didn't guess he could blame her. It was a gruesome and memorable sight.

He sighed. So many truly horrible things had happened to them since she'd returned to Adams. He wouldn't trade them for getting her back though. Hopefully the string of bad occurrences could stop once they were married. Who wanted to prevent their wedding?

Will went back into the house and locked the front door behind him. He donned his aviator jacket and a scarf from the hall tree. When would Beebe come home? Nothing was the same without that white ball of fluff bounding through the house. He'd check on him after he went to the project site. He grabbed his hardhat and steel toed boots from the garage.

Following the coordinates from Demeter, he arrived at a remote piece of land. He gathered his notes and legal pad and put on his hardhat. After taking a deep breath, he stepped out of the truck. Large trees hid a clearing. A shipping container sat off from the middle where an excavator was digging a huge hole to sink it into. The melting snow and ice made the ground squishy and muddy. The boots were handy as well as necessary to protect his feet.

"Another volunteer for the secret project, I presume?" The man appeared to be the foreman on the endeavor. "The quicker this is done, the sooner I'll have presents for my children."

Will nodded. "Guess we all have our price. I'm Will ..."

"No, don't tell me. When this hits the fan, I don't want to know anyone's name. All I need to know is what part of this project you are involved in."

"Air-handling, primarily."

"Oh, they want to breathe down there. Go figure." The man's mirthless laugh chilled Will. "One could only hope they'd go underground and suffocate, worthless scum."

"Not a fan?"

"Hardly. They've threatened my wife and kids. You're new, but they knew your price too." The man shook his head, then shrugged. "At least they pay well." He headed to the hole and talked with the heavy machinery operator.

Will made his way to the shipping container. Electricity had been run to it. The outside appeared to have been waterproofed with the exception of vent holes. That must be where he was to install some kind of ventilation system. The doors were open. Inside, someone had already installed shelving and drawers to stash whatever the shipment might be.

Like the foreman, he didn't want to know any more than he already did. He took some measurements to confirm the size of the space. Someone had already installed a hatch and ladder. Will climbed the ladder to be sure the hatch worked and was properly secured. He'd say this about Demeter and his crew, they hired people who did good work. Shame they were all beholden to criminals.

Kate greeted Sarah at the curb. "Good morning." Sarah handed her a list of stores in Clarksville to check for wedding dresses.

"I booked an appointment at three of these places. We can always cancel if we find something along the way." Sarah squealed. "I'm so excited to be part of this with you."

Kate wasn't excited. What if she was unable to find anything? "Be aware that I have no money to spend on this. It's a credit card purchase. Second, it has to be available by the twenty-third. We can't order and alter like most brides do." She climbed into the car and buckled her seatbelt.

"I don't think it will be a problem. Maybe they have stock to sell. Try to enjoy the experience." Sarah put the car in gear and raced away from the curb.

"I'd like to live through the experience, Sarah!" If

she had worn a hat, Kate would have been holding on to it.

After two stores and a stop for lunch, they arrived at the third appointment.

Kate exited the dressing room wearing yet another dress. They were all too expensive, but she had no choice but to go into debt for one. That is, if she found one that fit. No time for ordering a gown or for professional alterations. A thrift store or a vintage used clothing place was looking like her best hope.

"Oh, Katie! You look beautiful in that dress." Sarah clapped her hands. "Is this the one?"

She turned around. "It's held together with these big clips. No way to get it altered before Christmas.

The shop owner joined them. "Did you say by Christmas? There's no way to order you a gown by then, even if it fit perfectly!"

"Why am I trying on wedding dresses then?" Kate flung her hands in the air. "I'll go take this off." She slunked off to the dressing room.

"Kate, I have an idea." The shop owner stood behind her, taking off the clips and helping her out of the dress. "I don't know if it will fit, but we had a return. The wedding didn't occur, and the bride didn't want the dress hanging in her closet. We have a strict no return policy, especially after alterations, so she didn't get her money back. Are you interested in trying it on?"

"Sure, I have nothing to lose." Kate slipped on the robe provided by the dress shop and sat in the Queen Anne chair provided for brides. The enormity of the task overwhelmed her. The dress, the shoes, the pearls.

So much to replace in such a short time period.

"Katie?" A quiet knock on the fitting room door followed. "It's Sarah. Can I come in?"

Kate unlatched the door and returned to her seat.

Sarah entered and hugged Kate. "What will you do?"

"The shop owner is finding a dress that was returned. I guess we go to Goodwill next. Or I can sew something in my free time."

Sarah laughed. "Sounds like me. I bought an Easter dress pattern, fabric, even yarn to make a shawl. Three years ago. Easter came and went but no new dress. I cut it out last summer, still no new dress." She shrugged. "Maybe this year."

"Usher in the flying pigs, am I right?" Kate laughed with Sarah.

"Laughter is a sign of being uncomfortable." The shop owner came into the dressing room, carrying a dress made of lots of lace. "If you're invoking the flying pigs, well, I guess that's better than flying monkeys."

They all laughed.

The owner hung the dress on a hook on the wall. "What do you think of this?"

"Out of my price range. We saw it at another shop." Kate sighed. "We shouldn't take up any more of your time."

"Humor me and try it on."

Sarah went back to the showroom while the owner helped Kate put on the dress.

The sweetheart neckline and the buttoned-up back were a perfect fit. Ivory lace shimmered in the fluorescent lights. The lace sleeves came down to the back of her hand. The length was perfect for a moderate heel shoe.

"It's beautiful, but I can't afford it." Kate turned and looked at the back of the dress in the mirror. The train trailed behind her on the floor.

"It looks great on you. This dress has been paid for. It's just taking up space in my backroom. You'd be doing me a favor if you take it home with you."

"How much?" She loved it, and it fit as though it was made for her. She couldn't pay the price she'd seen on the same dress in a previous store.

"No charge. Take a look at the veils, sashes, or shoes. The dress is yours."

Gratitude and the sense of a God miracle occurring sent shivers through her. She swished the skirt back and forth. It was just what she'd buy if money was no object. "Okay! Thank you so very much."

"Go on out to the viewing area, and I'll gather some things that might go with it."

The owner headed out to the accessories. Kate went to the big mirrors where Sarah waited.

"Oh, Kate! It's beautiful, and it fits you perfectly, like it was made for you." Sarah made happy little claps. "Is she giving you a deal on it?"

Kate stepped onto the viewing platform that allowed the train to flow over it and onto the floor "Do you like it?"

"I love it on you. What about the cost? We saw the same dress at one of the other shops."

Kate whispered a word of wonder. "Free!"

Sarah squealed. "That's a God thing, isn't it?"

The owner came across the space with the matching veil and a pair of sparkly sandals. "What do you think of these?" She helped Kate with the veil. While Kate considered it, the owner ran across the shop to get the right size shoes for her to try on.

The dusty pink sandals with crystalline straps across her toes, diagonally across her foot, and around her ankle were both pretty and comfortable. In the end, she took the sandals and the free lace wedding gown.

They stopped by Chez Bell to store the wedding finery because Kate was afraid to take it to her own house. She could never feel certain her house was secure enough.

Chapter 17

Unraveling the mystery of the missing ring…

Kate waved good-bye to Sarah from the front porch of her house. After pulling the mail from the mailbox, she unlocked the deadbolt and the doorknob and entered, locking the door behind her. She hurried to enter the code to disable the security system before the wail of excruciating sound assaulted her eardrums. She hated the security system. She hated that she needed a security system.

More than that, she hated that she needed a security system that didn't seem to deter intruders.

The house was quiet, and Will seemed to still be out. Looking at the ceiling, she wondered, did mistletoe continue to grow after being cut down? Her ceiling seemed to have sprouted more greenery than she remembered from yesterday. Will had been at work.

Kate shook her head. He was wonderful and a little over the top on some things, and she'd loved him since she was five. She could hardly believe that in a little over two weeks they'd be married. After all they'd been through. It was a fairytale ending, or was it a beginning? She shrugged.

While flipping through the mail, make that bills, she found an oddly addressed envelope. She slit it open and pulled out the folded sheet of paper. Then she dropped it as though it was on fire. In bold black letters, it said, "DON'T MARRY WILL BELL!"

Andy was number three on speed dial behind Will and Maddy.

He answered on the first ring. "Katie? What's up?"

"My note writer uses the mail as well." Kate tried to control the shakiness in her voice. "I assume the Bell Witch wouldn't use the US Postal Service."

"Don't touch it any more than you must. I'll be right there."

Again. The sheriff's deputy was at her house more than Will was. This situation was unsustainable. Sheriff Davis would probably shut them down, so they wouldn't have to make a decision on what to do in January.

While she waited, Kate decided to go poke through the melting snow to see if she could find Will's missing ring. She doubted Brian had taken it. His approach was more smash and smash some more. He wouldn't have looked for the ring unless it just landed in his hand. Still …

When Andy pulled up, Kate was still poking around in the slushy snow and mud. But still no ring. She sighed.

"'Morning, Katie. Still looking for the ring?"

"No luck so far. Guess I need to clean up the mess in my room and hope it's still there." She hugged Andy. "Let's go in. I left the note where it fell."

Security chimes greeted them when they entered the house. She led Andy to the letter on the floor.

"There's the note. The envelope is on the desk."

Andy pulled on neoprene gloves before picking up the sheet of black lettering. "Here's what I don't understand. The message is clear, but why was it on the church walls? And, no offense, but when the person drugged Beebe, why didn't they drug you as well? You were asleep in the room. Why not harm you? Then there would be no wedding."

Kate shrugged. "I haven't heard from the vet. Guess I need to check on my poor puppy."

Andy slipped the letter and envelope into a Ziplock evidence bag. "I'll take this in and let forensics take a look for fingerprints. Keep all the doors locked when you don't have guests coming and going. Take this seriously. Should you cancel the wedding or move it to a more private location?"

The last thing she wanted to do was cancel the wedding. Moving it at this late hour with the church vandalized just wasn't feasible. That left a Justice of the Peace elopement at city hall. Not the way she saw that happening.

"No. I don't want to do that. Let's just catch the guy or gal, so we can go on about our lives." She paused. "You are keeping Will safe from his secret contract job, aren't you?"

"Doing what I can. I have TBI and the FBI working on that as well. Just keep the doors locked." He gave her a one-arm hug. "See you later."

Once he left, Kate started the linens washing, then she headed upstairs to recover her things. She brought up black trash bags to throw away all the damaged things and anything that was unnecessary.

The sliced-up wedding dress and shoes were the first things in the trash bag. No point grieving over what was ruined and over. She had a new dress and shoes at Chez Bell. All the police tape went in the bag next. Most of the shredded documents she could recover on her computer or get copies from the state.

Kate handled the broken glass from the pictures on her desk with care to avoid being cut. She slipped the pictures of her parents and Aunt Katharine out of the frames and into the desk drawer. She hovered with the frames over the trash bag. Yes, she could buy more glass, but that was just another hassle. She could also buy more frames. She tossed them into the trash.

The ledger she kept had been tossed across the room. Will kept records on his computer, but before he saw the bills and other expenses, Kate recorded them by hand in the ledger. After all, she was the one with a business degree. Yes, she knew they were drowning. Most small businesses struggled to make a profit in their first year of operation. That's why most of them failed. That and lack of capital to get them through the first year. Small business owners knew their specific business well, but they didn't know a thing about running a business, keeping records, and protecting their income stream. Now she was in the same boat as most small businesses. And it made her mad. She tucked the ledger into the top desk drawer and slammed it shut.

While she was at it, Kate culled the clothes and shoes in her closet. She didn't need the business outfits she'd bought to wear to work on Music Row. She kept ones she could wear to church or other dressier events. The rest went in a pile on her bed to donate. All the dressy shoes were unnecessary. She kept the ones that she could wear all day comfortably. The rest went on the bed. The old T-shirts, cut-offs, and ragged jeans she pitched. Worn out sneakers and sandals, pitched.

Eventually, Kate could see the floor, and the three black trash bags of refuse were stuffed full and tied. She bagged up the 'donate' pile on her bed then stuck a Post-it note on that bag that said 'DONATE'. Not much was left of the things she'd moved from Nashville. Someday she'd go shopping. Maybe during the after-Christmas sales.

Still no wedding ring though. Where could it be? Who would take it?

She dragged the bags to the hallway. She'd have to wait on Will to help her move them down the stairs.

The front door opened with the accompanying chimes. Then she heard the most welcome sound: woofing and scurrying dog feet!

"Beebe!"

Kate hurried down the stairs with the white ball of fluff coming up from the foyer. They met halfway on the staircase. She held the dog and wept with her face in his fur.

"There's no mistletoe there." Will sat on the step below Kate and Beebe.

"You know you can kiss me without mistletoe." Kate reached out and touched Will's shoulder. Beebe continued snuggling in her arms. "Did the vet have any instructions for Beebe?"

"Several things, one quite strange." Will took her hand and moved up beside her and Beebe. "Give him plenty of water. Don't be concerned if he doesn't eat much. Let him rest while the meds work their way out of his system."

"What was strange?" Kate had seen enough strange to last a lifetime.

"Dr. Bradley said someone had stolen all his ketamine. It's an anesthetic, but also used recreationally. He suspects that's what Beebe received. Thing is, there was more than the one dose Beebe got. Doc is required to keep a close watch on it since it is a Schedule III drug."

Kate's stomach dropped. "So, whoever took it has more to use indiscriminately."

"So, it would seem. I hear you received an interesting snail mail letter today." Will pulled her and Beebe closer. "I spoke with Andy on the way home, and he shared that information. He is sending the forensics team to check for fingerprints on Doc's medicine cabinet."

"He's probably wiped it down since the crime happened. At least, Beebe is home and happy to be here."

Will kissed her neck. "Did you find a dress you liked?"

"Yes! And it was free!" Kate kissed him. "We have more comfortable seating than the stairs, you know."

"We have a dinner engagement tonight at my brother Joe's house." Will squeezed her.

"Oh, do we dare leave the house and Beebe alone?" Kate held Beebe closer.

"I'll check with him and see if Beebe can come too." Will whipped out his phone. "Hey, Joe. ... Yeah, we're still on for dinner. ... Is it okay if we bring Beebe? We just got him back from the vet. ... He's fine. We just don't want to leave him alone. ... Great!"

"He said yes?" Kate's heart leapt.

"And he said we could come over whenever we're ready." Will hugged her. "I suggest we head over now."

Kate leaned over and whispered in his ear. "Could you get the trash bags down the stairs for me?"

Will laughed. "Of course, my love."

Chapter 18

Road to Christmas …

Will set the alarm and double-locked the front door while Katie and Beebe hurried out to the truck. Good thing Joe's house was close by. Having the "puppy" in the front seat between them would become close pretty quickly. Katie didn't say if she'd found the ring. She probably would have said if she had.

"You're going to need to move over, Beebe." Will scooted him over.

Katie laughed as the big puppy jumped into her lap. He hadn't heard her laugh in a long time. It made him smile. Tonight's meal would be a welcome relief from the daily craziness. Katie could hold baby Mandy and had her Beebe back. Both should help her feel better. She could also sleep in her own bed tonight if she wanted to do so.

He pulled the truck into Joe's driveway, setting off a series of barks from the house followed by howls from Beebe.

Will cringed. "This might not be such a good idea."

Katie jumped out of the truck, followed by Beebe on his leash. Before they reached the front door, Joe opened it and greeted them. Sally was right behind him, carrying baby Mandy.

They squeezed into the front hall and did the ballet of coat removals followed by the taking of the coats to the extra bedroom. Before Will knew what had happened, Katie had Mandy in her arms and was following Sally to the kitchen.

"Women and babies. Seems you can't have one without the other." Will shook his head.

"Not every woman gets to be a mom, though." Joe's expression was grim. "We tried to have a child for a while. We lost a couple in the process."

"I didn't know." Will wished he could withdraw the throwaway remark now that he did.

Joe put a hand on Will's shoulder. "Sally's pretty sensitive about it. I just didn't want you to say something and wish you hadn't."

"Already there, bro." Will shook his head. "Sorry to hear that. We haven't even talked about babies. We're still trying to get to the wedding." He shared their latest struggles with the house with Joe.

"Seems like as long as you invite strangers into the house and allow them to come and go, you'll always have the house open to security issues." Joe raised his eyebrows. "Know what I mean?"

Will rolled his eyes. "I do, actually. What do we do about it?"

"What about a combination keypad on the front door? You could change the code` every week."

Will scratched his chin. "That could work.

"What could work?" Katie entered the room *sans*

baby. "Sally's nursing and putting Mandy to bed. Dinner's done, just waiting for Mandy's needs to be met."

"Joe suggested a combination door lock for the front."

"Well, I hadn't thought of that. We could do the same for the root cellar door." Katie sat down on the arm of the sofa next to Will. Will wrapped his arm around her and pulled her close.

"Hey, no PDAs before the wedding!" Joe chuckled. "Seriously, how do you, you know, keep from giving into temptation living in that big house? Are you not attracted to each other in that way?"

Katie blushed and pulled away from him. "I'll go see what I can do for Sally."

Will scowled at his brother. "What is wrong with you? Of course, we're tempted to, you know, but we both are waiting for after the wedding. It's important to us both, and God helps us pull away when we're tempted. And I've only been in her room with her when the door is open and after one of these attacks. Not very tempting then."

Joe raised his hands in surrender. "Okay, okay. I'm just teasing you. I just remember how hard it was for Sally and me."

Will grinned. "I never said it was easy, but with all that's happened, I need to be on the premises to keep her safe."

Joe's Weimaraner Rochester ran through to the basement with Beebe just behind him.

"Looks like Beebe's back to his old self." Joe scrunched his eyebrows together. "Who would try to hurt him and Katie?"

Will shrugged. "If you have any ideas, I'm open to hearing them."

Sally called out from the kitchen. "Dinner is ready, guys."

After playing Rook for a while, guys against girls, the clock in the living room chimed eleven times.

"Time to go. I turn into a pumpkin soon." Katie stood and stretched. "I did find a new wedding dress and shoes today. I also got the mess in my room cleaned up. I'm beat."

Joe got their coats from the extra bedroom. The girls hugged, then Joe helped Katie with her coat.

"This was fun. We should make dinner and cards a regular event." Sally hugged Will.

"That sounds great. It's nice to be out of the house for a while. Beebe, come."

Ferocious sounds came tearing up the stairs with both dogs fighting for dominance. Beebe ran to Katie and sat for his leash.

"Good dog." She clipped it on him. "See you guys soon."

After another round of good-byes, 'cause it's the South, they climbed into the truck. A few minutes later, Will pulled up in front of the B&B. They laughed and snuggled while Beebe pulled on his leash to the front porch. Beebe whined and cried and wouldn't go up onto the porch.

Katie squatted down in front of him. "What's wrong, sweet dog?"

"I can't believe this." Will pulled out his phone and snapped a picture of the front door and sent it to Andy.

Katie stood and walked over to Will's side, pulling the dog up the stairs.

"Our wedding un-planner paid us another visit."

On the door, a knife impaled another sheet of paper with the same warning. "DON'T MARRY WILL BELL."

Kate shrank away from the front door. Will wrapped his arms around her. Kate buried her face into his flannel shirt.

"This is a nightmare, Will. Why don't they want us to marry?"

Will kissed the top of her head. "Andy's on his way with the forensics team, so he doesn't want us to enter the house. I should take you and Beebe to Mom and Dad's again."

"No. It's my house after all. I need to know if someone has entered and damaged something." Kate crossed her arms.

Beebe whined and stood on his hind legs braced against Kate.

Will petted the dog. "I know, Beebe. Whoever it is came back."

Beebe got down and began sniffing around on the porch and the front door. Then he pulled Kate down the steps and around the house to the backyard. She opened the gate, and Beebe pulled the leash out of her hand and began running in circles near the root cellar door.

Will closed the gate and followed Kate and Beebe

to the root cellar. He shrugged and pulled out his key to the lock. But he didn't need a key because the lock was open, and the door was ajar. Will flung the door open.

Kate grabbed on to Will's arm. "Andy said not to go in."

He caressed her hand. "If I don't go in now, we may miss the opportunity to catch the person responsible."

She sighed. "Okay. Take Beebe with you. I'll go sit in the truck to wait for Andy."

Will and Beebe disappeared into the dark root cellar. Kate walked back around to the front, climbed into the truck, and locked the doors. She sat there for what felt like forever, but then she heard a pounding on the hood. The windshield had fogged over with her breath. Kate opened the door and stepped out. The stranger turned and ran off into the dark.

Andy's deputy car pulled up as the person disappeared into the night. "Where's Will?"

"In the house through the root cellar. The lock was open, so Will went in with Beebe."

"Not surprised. Key?"

Kate handed him her keys. "Someone banged on the hood before heading down the street."

"Good. Maybe there will be fingerprints. Stay here." Andy stomped toward the front porch.

Chapter 19

Second weekend in December …

Will helped Beebe down the ladder-like steps into the root cellar and then up the rickety stairs into the first-floor inner hallway. Beebe sniffed in the dust and sneezed. Then he took off through the dark. Will took a moment to grab a flashlight from inside the butler's pantry, then hurried to follow the dog. Beebe sniffed at the alcove opening and scratched at the wood floor.

Will released the door into the foyer. Beebe bolted right into Andy's legs and whimpered.

"Which part of 'stay out of the house' sounded open to interpretation?" Andy flipped on a light and glared at Will. "Now the dog has messed up whatever clues were in the dust of the secret passageway, and you've added your own later fingerprints to the lock on the root cellar. Not only that, but you left Katie alone in the truck with only door locks to keep her safe. Shattering a window would leave her defenseless when the intruder came out and banged on the hood of the truck!"

"Andy, I …"

"No, Officer Lawrence to you right now. I represent the law." Andy's face was stern and angry. "I could arrest you for entering the house after I ordered you to stay out. Here's what you're going to do: take Katie to your mom's and stay there until morning. I'll call you tomorrow about whatever we find."

Will saluted Andy. "Yes, sir, Officer Lawrence. Come on, Beebe." He slammed the front door as he left the house. *In Katie's and my own house! How dare he kick me out?* Luckily, Beebe's crate was still in the truck bed.

He and Beebe climbed into the truck next to Katie. Then Will slammed the door

"What happened?" Katie's voice was small and shaky.

"Andy pulled rank on me and kicked me out of our house! Then he told me to take you and Beebe to Mom's and stay there until morning." He slammed his hand onto the steering wheel.

"Well, he did tell you not to enter the house, but you did. Someone came out of the house and slammed their hand onto the hood of the truck."

"Who was it? Could you tell?" Will felt terror that Katie had been alone with the intruder again.

Katie shook her head. "Andy did say he wanted to try to get fingerprints from the hood."

Will called Andy again.

"What now?" Andy rarely got mad, but his temper could be explosive.

"Do you want me to wait for forensics to get the fingerprints from the hood of my truck?"

Silence. "Yes, wait for forensics."

In preparing for the second weekend of December, Kate took Will's advice and made the activities more self-directed.

In the foyer, she set up the wrapping station with colorful paper, ribbon, bows, and tags. From the bountiful supply of mistletoe, Kate even appropriated sprigs to tie onto packages. Tape, markers, and scissors in a Santa mug completed the arrangement on the long hall table.

In the sitting room, she piled Christmas books. Children's books included Dr. Suess's *How the Grinch Stole Christmas*, Charles Schulz's *A Charlie Brown Christmas*, Clement C. Moore's *A Visit from St. Nicholas*, and Barbara Shook Hazen's *Rudolph the Red-Nosed Reindeer*. For older kids and kids at heart, Kate provided Dickens's *A Christmas Carol* in various versions. She also laid out a Bible and the nativity verses from her mom's old Bible.

On the piano, Kate provided Christmas sheet music and a Reader's Digest compendium of Christmas songs.

Opposite the burgundy settee, Will helped her set up a TV over the fireplace and a Blu-ray player with a selection of Christmas movies: *Holiday Inn*, *It's a Wonderful Life*, several versions of *A Christmas Carol* (including the Muppets), *Rudolph the Red-Nosed Reindeer*, *A Charlie Brown Christmas*, and *The Holiday* for the ladies. Will insisted on a copy of *Die Hard* along with a discussion of whether or not it was a Christmas movie at all. They added chairs and bean bags for the children and teens.

In the kitchen, Kate had baked Christmas sugar cookies and provided decorating options: icing in red, white, and green, Christmasy sprinkles, and red and green miniature M&Ms.

For breakfast, she had strudel from Sarah's Bakery, cinnamon rolls, Pluck-it Cake (also called Monkey Bread), and breakfast casserole. She also fixed a charcuterie board with cured meats, cheeses, and fruit. Kate purchased various kinds of crackers to go with it.

She filled holiday dishes with Christmas candy: chocolate bells, peppermint candy canes, old-fashioned ribbon candy, and chocolate-covered cherries. Aunt Katharine and Grandma's Christmas glassware and china completed the decorations.

Before the guests arrived, Kate noticed Andy pull up in his squad car. He was in uniform but took off his cap when he reached the front door. Kate threw open the door and pulled him inside. Then she gave him a bear hug.

Andy blushed. "Wow, that's a better greeting than I expected or deserved. Is Will around?"

"He's out in the garage working on his secret project." Kate stepped back from their friend. If he was here about that, then he wouldn't be there to see her. "I hoped you knew something from Monday night."

"The only thing I know for sure is that every one of the notes you've received was printed on the same printer from the same file. They're identical. We didn't get recognizable fingerprints. The person either isn't in the system, or their prints were unclear to the computer." Andy shook his head. "I thought there was a chance at a clear, usable print but apparently not."

"Did you notice the new keypad lock on the front door?" Kate opened the door to show him. "We can reset the combination every week for guests and have a master combination for us."

"Good idea. Who thought of that?" Andy turned his hat around and around.

"Joe." Kate felt uncomfortable because Andy was so uncomfortable. "You know, there's no reason to be nervous with me or Will. You were doing your job. We appreciate all the time and energy our situation has taken."

"Still, I shouldn't have blown up at Will. Is it okay if I go back and talk with him?"

Kate nodded. "Of course. You're his oldest friend."

"No." Andy grinned. "You are his oldest and dearest friend."

It was Kate's turn to blush it seemed since the heat of it scorched her face. "Not the same, Andy."

He hugged her and headed back through the house to go to the garage.

Will jumped at the knock on the garden door. He peered out the small window and saw Andy waiting there. He unlocked the multiple locks he'd installed and opened the door.

"Andy! I was wondering if you were ever coming back." Will slapped him on the back and invited him in. "What do you know?"

"Nothing. Fingerprints were a bust. Even the

security footage was hard to make out." He sat in the chair in front of Will's desk. "Your intruder is probably a woman, too short to be easily found by the security camera. Beyond that, I'm stymied."

"What about that other matter?" Will raised his eyebrows, trying to remind Andy that the garage could be bugged.

Andy shrugged. "Feds are involved."

Will nodded. "Got it. About the other night …"

"Done and done." Andy raised his eyebrows. "I was overtired and took your disregard for my instructions too seriously. I've known you most of your life. When did you ever do what I asked?"

Will gave a short laugh. "Well, there's that."

The alarm went off on Will's phone. "Three o'clock. We have guests coming. I don't like to have Katie greet them alone. After all, we don't run background checks on these people."

Andy shook his head. "Maybe you should."

Chapter 20

Another Christmasy weekend …

Kate was determined to remain in the background during this weekend because she was exhausted, and the guests didn't come to see her but to be involved with their own families. To that end, she had fixed up the stations with things to do at the house, and she provided a map and a list of local places to go to eat. The weather was better, so going out for lunch and dinner wasn't as difficult. Christmas shopping in Springfield or Clarksville was also an option.

She walked through the downstairs, making sure all was ready.

When the security chimes sounded, Kate hurried to the foyer to greet the guests.

The first to arrive was a couple with two young children. The man greeted her. "Hi, are you Kate?"

"I am. You must be John and Michelle Larrabee. Introduce me to the rest of your family."

Michelle pulled the children forward though the girl held onto her mom's leg and a doll. "The clinger is Hattie, aged four, and her brother Jeffrey is seven."

Hattie looked up at Kate with large green eyes and gave a timid smile. "My baby is named Violet."

Kate squatted down to her eye level. "What a wonderful name, Miss Hattie. You have an interesting name too."

Hattie smiled and let go of her mom's leg. "Do you have a little girl I can play with?"

"No, but other guests have children, too, this weekend."

The little girl came toward Kate, tentatively at first, then she threw her arms around Kate's neck. Kate held the warm little girl.

"Wow! You must have angel dust because she never warms up to anyone that fast."

She hugged Hattie back and then stood. Her back couldn't handle picking up random guests after her fall in the attic during the summer.

The boy approached Kate and stuck out his hand. "I'm Jeffrey. I'm seven."

She shook his hand. "Glad to meet you. I hope you have a good time with us."

Retreating to the desk, Kate rifled through the packets for this weekend and pulled out theirs. "I have your packet right here. You're in number five. It has more room for the rollaway bed and your Pack 'n' Play. In your packet, you have gift cards to a couple of restaurants and a map with other places highlighted. I also noted some interesting places to shop. I'll have breakfast each morning, and some snacks available as you need them during the day. You can come and go through the front door combination lock using the code on a card in your packet."

"Wow! You've thought of everything." Michelle

took the packet from Kate.

"I've set up stations for various Christmas activities. We have books and movies, Christmas music for the piano, and cookie decorating. There's even a wrapping station." She pointed to the Victorian sideboard (with a glass topper to protect the antique) and all the wrapping needs. "Let me know how I can help you have a wonderful weekend."

Michelle picked up Hattie. "Thank you, Kate. What a beautiful house! We'll just go settle into our room for now."

Hattie waved to Kate as her mom carried her up the stairs.

Will came into the foyer as John was picking up their luggage and the Pack 'n' Play. "Let me help. I'm Will, Katie's fiancé." Will grabbed the extra bags and headed up the stairs with John.

"Thanks for the help. I'm John. I'd shake your hand, but …"

Will laughed. "Later."

Kate smiled. Will did such a good job of making people feel at ease, an important skill for an innkeeper.

When the front door opened again, her second family stepped in. Parents and young teenagers entered the foyer.

"Hi, I'm Kate." She smiled and hurried to shake the father's and mother's hands.

"Jules and Martha Brooks. These are our teens, Joseph and Marlon." The boys were typically sullen and acting as though they wanted to be anywhere else.

"Welcome. You booked two rooms, number three and number four. There's a rollaway bed in number four to give your boys their own beds." Kate explained her plans for the weekend like she had for the Larrabees.

"What movies do you have? Anything we'd want to see." The older teen crossed his arms in a challenge. "Probably just Rudoph and St. Nick."

"There's *The Muppet Christmas Carol* and *Die Hard* and others."

Marlon hit his brother in the shoulder. "Those are cool."

Joseph nodded. "Cool, cool."

Martha mouthed, 'Thank you.'

Jules handed each boy a suitcase. "Go up the stairs. Adjust your attitude before we go somewhere for dinner."

"Pizza, Dad. Pizza." Joseph and Marlon nodded.

"We'll see." Jules picked up the remaining luggage.

As the Brooks family climbed the stairs, the front door opened a third time.

Kate greeted them at the door. "Welcome, you must be the Morans, Ben and Erica with Mariane."

Ben had the young girl in his arms, sleeping. "She passed out after lunch and slept the rest of the way."

"That's okay. There's another young girl here this weekend. I bet they'll be fast friends." Kate handed Erica their packet.

"That's good. See, babe, it will be okay." Erica patted his arm.

Kate smiled. "The rollaway bed is already in the room if you'd like to go on up and lay her down."

"Go ahead, Ben. I'll get our information." Erica handed him the room key.

Will came down the stairs and took the key from

Ben to help him get Mariane settled in room two.

When all was set upstairs, Will found Kate in the kitchen and leaned on the counter as she worked to prepare dinner for the two of them. "I need to go out to the construction site to see about installing the unit that came today. If it fits and works, this contract will be fulfilled."

Kate exhaled. "That would make life better."

Will nodded. "Are you okay? I feel like you've withdrawn from me." He reached for her and drew her to him. "We're getting married in two weeks. What's going on?"

"It's just so much. The intruders, the destruction of my things, and the loss of your ring. I think I'm just weary." Kate wrapped her arms around him. "I'm not unsure about the wedding. In some ways, I've imagined that day since we were children."

Will kissed her. "Hang in there with me, Katie. I'd hate to lose you when we're so close to our future together."

"I'm not letting go. I just had to set it all aside to prepare for this weekend." Kate kissed him back. "I still wonder who knows me well enough to destroy my dress and shoes and take your ring. Whoever it is despises me to put me through this madness."

Will leaned his forehead on hers. "Stay with me, Katie. We can only defeat the madness together."

She nodded and gave in to his arms. "I love you, Will Bell. Could there really be a Bell Witch that's bedeviling us?"

"No. I don't believe she, it, exists." As he said this, a door slammed upstairs. He jumped then gripped her tighter. "That doesn't mean we're not in danger. I'm more concerned about the biker gang I'm working for than I am about a historical bogeyman."

She tried to relax in his arms. "Be careful at the work site. Dinner at five-thirty?"

"I'll see you then." Will kissed her nose and then her lips.

Dread filled Kate with fear. Surely, she had no reason to fear today over any other day in recent history. They'd come through worse events since she moved to Adams, Tennessee.

Chapter 21

Missing Will …

Five-thirty came and went while Kate waited for Will to come back. When the cuckoo sounded six, she packed up dinner into containers and placed it all in the refrigerator, so the kitchen would be clear for cookie decorating when the families returned. Kate didn't eat because she was worried that something had happened.

She retired to the sitting room to read her latest book. At six-thirty, the Morans returned and retired to their room.

The Brooks returned as the cuckoo sounded seven.

Joseph, the older teen boy, came to Kate. "Is it okay to watch a movie now? Is there microwave popcorn and soda?"

Kate smiled. "Yes, to all three as long as your parents are okay with it."

Jules Brooks stuck his head in the sitting room. "Sounds like a great plan. I'll be back down to join them once I change into sweats. Martha's feeling tired. She'll probably just chill in the room to read her new book."

Marlon punched Joseph's shoulder. "Sweats? Yes, please." The boys pounded up the steps.

After helping the Brooks men start *Die Hard*, complete with popcorn and Coke, Kate heard the cuckoo at seven-thirty. Still no Will. Should she call Andy?

She tried Will's phone. No answer. Her heart felt like it would burst from her chest.

Kate phoned Andy.

"Katie? What's going on now?"

"Will was supposed to be home for dinner at 5:30. That was two hours ago." Tears ran down her face. "I just tried his phone, but he didn't answer."

"Was he going to the mysterious work site?"

His concerned tone calmed her. "Yes. Do you know where it is?"

"No. He didn't tell me, and we've not discovered it yet."

Kate swallowed. "What do I do?"

Just then the front door opened and closed. Will joined Kate in the sitting room. He wrapped his arms around her. "I'm so sorry, Sweetheart. I'm so sorry."

She handed him her phone. "It's Andy."

"False alarm, friend. I was detained at the site, then my phone was dead when I had a flat tire."

Kate snuggled into Will's flannel shirt and open aviator jacket, wrapping her arms around him as well. Inhaling his masculine scent and woodsy cologne, she closed her eyes and thanked God Will was safe in her arms. Then she was mad.

"Bye, Andy. Enjoy your evening. We're fine here." He hung up and snuggled into her shoulder.

"Are we fine?" She kept her voice low, so they couldn't be heard over the movie playing in the next room. "How could you go out and not have a full charge on your phone? Why didn't you plug it into the truck jack and call me? I was worried sick that the biker gang had killed you."

"Shush, shush, shush. Everything is okay, Katie-girl." He hugged her close to him. "I'm sorry to have worried you. I had taken the charging cord out of the truck for someone else to use at the site, then I forgot to get it back from him. How was I to know I'd picked up a nail in a tire?"

Kate truly wanted to hit him, so he'd feel the pain she felt in her heart. But with guests in the next room, movie or no, she didn't want to air her grievances for strangers to hear. She chose to hold in her anger, for now. "Did you eat?"

"Actually, the guy who helped me with the tire brought me a burger, fries, and a Coke."

Kate closed her eyes and seethed while holding him close.

"You didn't eat waiting for me, right?"

She nodded. If she opened her mouth, unrighteous things might escape at a high volume.

"I'll go put on more comfortable clothes, then let me help you get something to eat." Will released his hold on her, and she did the same. "I'm in deep trouble, aren't I?

"Yes." Kate stressed the 's' sound. "The guys in the living room are wearing sweats and watching *Die Hard*."

"Great! Sweats it is." Will hurried out into the garden to change in the garage.

Kate sank into her favorite chair in the sitting room. For him, the whole event was done and over, but she still felt the stabbing pain in her heart. What Will didn't know was that since her heart attack in the ambulance after breaking her back, she had been taking medication to prevent another heart attack. Kate needed to tell him that her heart was a ticking time bomb. She released the breath she'd seemed to have been holding all evening. "Thank you, God, for keeping him safe. Help me feel joy that he's back and soothe the anger I feel in his lackadaisical attitude about it. Give me the words to tell him about my heart condition before our wedding."

Jules Brooks poked his head into the sitting room. "Is there more popcorn and soda?"

Kate nodded. "I'll get it for you." She stood and headed to the kitchen while Mr. Brooks rejoined his sons. She smiled. This scene was what she pictured when planning to run a bed and breakfast. Though probably without *Die Hard*. It soothed her heart for the moment, and she went to pop more corn and gather more soda from the fridge.

Will turned on the light for the backyard and plunged into the night. His heartbeat sped up as he reviewed the experiences of the evening. He'd tell Kate more once she got over being worried and angry over his lateness. After unlocking the door's multiple locks, he plunged into darkness until he located the wall switch. He poked around the space, including the side with Kate's new car, looking for Demeter or one of his gang members.

Slipping off his coat and shirt, he opened the underbed drawer and pulled out a long sleeve t-shirt with *Lord of the Rings* quotes on it and a pair of sweatpants.

Things had not gone well at the site. The shipping container was already in the hole in the ground, making it nigh on impossible to mount the air transfer system on the outer part of the container. The unit he'd acquired for said purpose would not work without being able to mount it on the outside. Now he needed to purchase a different unit small enough to fit down the hatch. Then he had to find a way to vent and to pull outside air into the container.

He pulled on the shirt and sweats and stowed the clothes he took off in another underbed drawer. He pulled on his jacket and headed back through the night to the house.

Of course, Demeter and his thugs had been on site to see how things were going. The man gave Will the willies. Demeter was not happy with most of what he saw and made threats to all the workers on site and to all their families. He made it quite clear that if the project was not complete by Christmas, St. Nick would not be the only surprise visitor on Christmas morning.

Twenty-five thousand dollars was not worth the worry, pain, and suffering this job would cause if he couldn't fulfill the contract. Will couldn't leave Kate as a widow three days after the wedding. He took a deep breath of frosty night air. He let it out slowly then plastered a grin on his face. *Die Hard* awaited. It was probably the only way he'd get to watch this movie before Christmas.

A movement in the shadows startled him. A cat's meow made Will laugh. Jumping at shadows. Demeter's threats were effective. Could he order an appropriately sized unit and install it in less than two weeks? He hoped so, but he severely doubted it.

He climbed the steps to the kitchen door, then he took another deep breath. Kate didn't need to see his fear.

Chapter 22

Saturday activities …

As soon as she opened the door to her bedroom onto the landing, Kate smelled fresh brewed coffee and breakfast casserole. Will was up. Beebe tore down the steps to find him. A stroke of anger still bedeviled her. With all the stuff that had gone on with the house and each other, how could he think he could leave the house without a charge on his phone?

When she reached the foyer, she saw the two young girls playing in the sitting room with their dolls. Hattie's brother Jeffrey was coloring in a coloring book.

"Hi, Miss Kate!" Was that Mariane or Hattie? "I like your puppy dog."

"Hi, Miss Kate!" The other young girl greeted her.

"I confess. I didn't pay close enough attention when you checked in yesterday. Which of you had Miss Violet as a name for her dolly?" Kate squatted down to them.

The blonde girl raised her hand.

"That makes you Hattie, right?"

She clapped her hands in joy. "And that's my brother, Jeffrey."

He smiled and waved then went back to his art project.

"Mariane, I didn't meet your baby doll. What's her name?"

The dark-haired girl ran up to Kate and held out a well-loved doll. "This is Margaret."

Kate shook the doll's hand. "Good morning, Margaret. Did you and Mariane sleep well last night?"

"Oh, yes, ma'am." Mariane spoke in a high-pitched doll voice then giggled at her doll's response.

"Breakfast smells oh so good. When will it be ready? Violet's getting hungry." Hattie rocked her baby.

"We'll have to ask Will because he's the one who got up early to start it." Kate grinned.

"A boy making breakfast? That doesn't happen at my house."

A giggle from behind Kate was from her mom Michelle. "Now Hattie, Daddy makes you pancakes sometimes. Jeffrey often helps with lunches and dinner."

Hattie scrunched her shoulders. "Yes, I guess a boy can make breakfast."

Mariane and Hattie ran into the kitchen together, holding hands.

"Good morning, Michelle. How is everything going?" Kate smiled.

Michelle grinned. "My husband is having a hard time waking up. If Erica hadn't told us Marianne was up playing with her doll, I'd have made him come downstairs with her.

Erica brought two cups of coffee from the kitchen to the table. "Just in time for coffee, Michelle. Good morning, Kate. Your Will is a true treasure. Never let him go."

"Oh, I know it." Kate hurried into the kitchen to find her treasured man.

"Coffee, Lovely Lady?"

Will's smile melted her heart. It was hard to stay mad at him.

"You know I do." Kate slipped her arms around his waist as he poured her cup. "I'm told by one of our lady guests that you are a treasure."

"Some people will say anything for a cup of coffee." He put the pot down and hugged her closer. "Good morning, Sweetheart. I love you." Will bent down for a kiss.

Kate returned his kiss. "I know. I was so worried last night. I wasn't very loving, but I'm afraid. Between the intruder and your secret contract …"

He laid his head on hers. "Darling, I promise to be very careful with these thugs. Nothing, I mean absolutely nothing, will keep me from marrying you on the twenty-third."

Kate smiled at his optimism, a quality she found hard to hold onto since living in Adams. She always felt there was another shoe to drop, and she was just waiting for the thud. Was the Bell Witch real and bedeviling her? Was the Witch sending her messages? From a printer? Unlikely, even if the Bell Witch was real.

Will nuzzled her hair.

Kate loved him so very much. "I would marry you today, despite the messages and the creep factor. I'm sure that would not make some folks happy. But the twenty-third is soon enough. And neither one of us would ever forget our anniversary."

Erica poked her head around the swinging door to the kitchen. "Okay if I serve the casserole for the girls, Michelle, and me."

Kate untangled from Will's embrace. "No, you're on vacation. I can serve you. How much do the girls want?"

She served her guests and helped carry plates to the table. When she returned to the kitchen, Kate found a cup of coffee, just the right color, a plate with casserole and croissant, and a card sitting on the table. She slit the envelope with a knife. She read the note inside the card and nearly cried.

"You haven't seen the best part yet. Take another look in the envelope." He looked just like a child at Christmas who can't wait to open his gifts.

Kate opened the envelope to see plane tickets to Scotland. "Oh, my! How?"

"The MacGowan family sent them for our honeymoon for Christmas through Hogmanay! They also set us up in a cottage on the MacGowan estate with a car to use."

Behind each ticket was cash in British pound sterling. Tears poured forth in earnest. They would have a real honeymoon adventure from guests who had had a horrible weekend plus longer at their B&B. And the new MacGowan leader, a teenager, had told Kate that the Bell Witch had told him to warn her not to marry Will Bell. Maybe he thought he could spare them by whisking them out of the country. Kate nodded to herself. *Why not?*

"Earth to Katie, earth to Katie." Will sat beside her waving his hand in front of her face. "What are you thinking, sweet Katie?"

"That we are blessed with good friends with whom we survived a horrific week." She gave Will a look she hoped said how much she loved him.

He kissed her hand. "They sent all the pieces to me to put together for you."

"It's fantastic. I hadn't thought much about a honeymoon. I figured we'd do well to have a week or so here without strangers." Kate squeezed his hand.

"Darling, wherever we are together is heaven on earth." He checked the time. "I have a Zoom meeting this morning at nine. I'll see you in a little while."

"Did you eat?" She called after him.

"Leftover cake from last weekend." He winked and waved, then plunged out into the garden area.

Will had failed to pick up his leather jacket on the way out the door. He shivered and scuttled to the garden door to the garage. He was well and truly frozen by the time he unlocked the bolts on the door. The office was warmer than the outside temperature, but the garage wasn't well enough insulated for long-term human dwelling. He dug through the drawers under the bed and found a heavy sweater to help him warm up.

After starting a K-cup, he logged on and brought up the Zoom account. He went back for the cup of hot coffee and returned to see his conference partner had also logged on.

"Will Bell. What's going on with your big

contract?" Anthony, his 'friend' from the Nashville engineering firm, filled the screen.

"Nothing good, friend." Will kept his face from sneering. "What did you promise them?"

"A working air transfer system so they can stay in the container if they need to hide out for a while. Why? Is there some kind of problem?" Anthony's mug filled the screen. It read, 'Do unto others before they do unto you.'

Will shook his head. "They dropped the container into the hole before I got the unit attached. Everyone knows their own job but not anyone else's. What am I going to do now?"

Anthony shrugged. "Get it fixed by Christmas. These guys aren't playing. Why do you think I passed on it? I've got kids that need their Daddy for Christmas." He laughed.

"You're despicable. What kind of role model are you to your children?"

Anthony sipped his coffee. "Listen, they're small. I have time to clean up my role model. You didn't call this meeting to insult me, did you?"

Will chewed the inside of his cheek. "No, I need some help."

During the remainder of the hour, Anthony and Will discussed the pros and cons of various other units and the ways to attach them to the inside of the container.

"Thanks for talking it over with me. None of the contractors talk to one another. That's how my unit got messed over." Will drummed with the end of a pencil.

"Like you, they've been told not to tell anyone about their contracts." He shrugged. "I gotta go take my two to Nashville for shopping and lunch. Gag me."

"That's fine. Bye." Will closed the Zoom meeting window. What was he doing, chancing everything for $25,000? They'd just as likely kill him as pay him. A trip to Scotland was just the ticket to get Katie and him out of the country and the reaches of Demeter and his thugs.

Chapter 23

Winding up weekend number two …

The Brooks boys watched a lot more television, videos, and football than Kate would have allowed on a family vacation. Most of the time, Jules joined them, leaving Martha to wrap presents and decorate cookies alone. The rest of the time she spent in their room or in the sitting room reading her book. She could have done all of that at home.

Michelle and Erica bonded over their little girls. Their husbands hung out with the other men watching television.

Kate was disturbed at how the family dynamics worked, or didn't, with the addition of the TV in the living room. However, she had promised herself and Will to stay out of the choices each family made. By Saturday afternoon, Kate needed to disrupt the activity, or not activity, going on in her house. She climbed the stairs to the attic and rummaged through boxes.

"Katie, what are you doing?"

Kate dropped the box she was holding and whirled around, fully expecting the Bell Witch.

It was Will. "Sorry, I didn't mean to startle you." He stepped to her side and picked up the box and its contents. "But I still wonder what you're up to."

"Will! You scared the daylights out of me." Her voice was shaky, and her nerves danced as though electrified. "I'm looking for a game the guys could interact around. You know, Monopoly, Risk, Battleship."

He grinned. "Thought you were going to let them do what they were going to do this weekend."

"But they're not doing anything with their families. At least the little girls could watch *The Muppet Christmas Carol* if the guys did something else." Kate crossed her arms. "I'm not trying to be judge-y, but it looks like a middle school dance right now, the men in one corner and the ladies in another."

Will's rumbly laugh filled the attic. "You'd make a great cruise activities director. I think we stashed those games in the hall closet with office supplies and such."

Kate brightened. "You're right. I remember that now."

"Can you say that again so I can record it?" Will pulled his phone from a pocket, opened the camera, and began videoing Kate.

"What do you want me to say?" Kate furrowed her forehead. "You're right?"

"That's it. It may be the only time I'm right, so I need a record of the event."

Kate put up her hand. "Stop. You're right a lot of the time."

"Ooh. That's even better." He stopped the recording. "I'm just kidding. I'll go get the games and put them on the dining table. Then they can choose to do game night, or not."

"Thank you." Kate sulked. "I don't rule the roost here, you know. I care a lot about what you want."

Will put his arms around her. "I know. I'm just teasing you." He kissed her cheek and headed back down the stairs.

Kate looked around the attic, at the scars from the fire and the new lumber from the roof repair, the trunks of stuff, the old rocking chair. As a child, this attic was the backdrop for her favorite playtimes on rainy days. Last summer ex-boyfriend Brian had scared her witless with his interpretation of the Bell Witch haunting up here and locked her in. She'd fallen down the stairs to the safe room in the center of the house, breaking her back in several places causing the resulting heart attack on the way to the hospital. In one of these trunks, she'd found Great-Aunt Katharine's lace wedding dress, which was shredded by the intruder and was in a black trash bag now.

She breathed a deep sigh then headed back down the stairs to her guests.

In the sitting room, she placed a card table with six chairs. She spread a Christmas tablecloth. Then she placed Aunt Katharine's Christmas tea dishes on the table. A three-tiered graduated serving tray held Christmas cookies, sponge cake, and shortbread. The teapot held steaming blackberry-sage tea. The sugar and creamer set completed the table. She rang the dinner bell to summon the ladies to a three o'clock tea party.

"Oh, my! This is beautiful!" Erica waved the other ladies into the sitting room. "Look at how amazing this looks." She pulled out her phone and took pictures. She had Mariane sit down and helped her choose her sweets. Then she took a picture of her lifting her teacup.

The other ladies filled in the spots with Hattie across from Mariane. Kate took the remaining position on a corner of the square table as the 'pourer of the tea.' The little ladies received a small amount of tea. All of them took samples of all of the sweets.

The Brooks boys entered the sitting room.

"Cool! Cookies!" Marlon, the younger boy, reached for the treats.

Martha Brooks slapped his hand. "Boys, unless you plan to have tea with us, you'll have to wait and see if any of the goodies remain."

"Aw, Mom!" Joseph leaned against the entry woodwork. "Why can't we just get some now? We'll take them into the other room."

"Yeah, we don't need any tea." Marlon held his hand, nursing the slap.

"This is a proper tea party for girls." Mariane lifted a cookie and bit into it.

"Yeah, you're boys, so you're not allowed." Hattie took a bite of her shortbread.

Kate smiled at the young girls. "The boys can join if they want to sit with us. I can get two more chairs."

The boys looked at each other.

Joseph became the spokesman for them. "Nah. We'll eat leftovers later."

The tea party only lasted thirty minutes, but everyone enjoyed the break in the afternoon.

When it was over, Kate filled the treat tray and placed it on the dining room table next to the games Will had retrieved from the hall closet. The lure worked! The boys came for the cookies; the men, including Will, started the Monopoly game.

In the sitting room, Kate read in her favorite chair. The girls played with their dolls while the moms conversed. She heard the rumble as the men and boys came into the small parlor.

Jules Brooks headed the herd. "We're ordering pizza if it's okay. Will says there's a place that delivers here."

Kate assumed the conversation was meant for the ladies who were their guests, so she continued reading.

"Katie, is it okay?" Will was the one with the pleading eyes at the doorway.

She looked up at him. "You don't need my permission. These ladies need dinner too. They should have input."

"Is it okay, Mom?" Marlon came closer to his mom.

Martha looked around at the other women. Erica and Michelle shrugged.

"Sure, why not?"

The men cheered, and Will got out his phone to call Angelo's. He brought up the website with the menu, and the men retired to the dining room to order pizza.

Martha stood. "I better guide the ordering. Trust me, with two teenaged boys, there's no telling what they'll end up ordering. What would the girls and Jeffrey prefer?"

"Cheese and pepperoni?" Erica checked with Michelle who nodded.

"Okay, one stripped down pizza for the smaller kids." Martha hurried to put in her guidance.

When the pizza arrived, Kate provided paper plates and soda.

The little girls and the moms retired to the living room to watch *The Muppet Christmas Carol* while the men played Monopoly. Jeffrey didn't want to get stuck with the girls, so he played Monopoly with his dad. When the movie concluded, the females all retired to bed. Kate put away the leftovers and threw away the fancy paper dishware.

Will was winning when Kate called it a night.

Chapter 24

Finding a ring …

The three families left before nine, so Will and Kate dressed for church services.

Kate ran around the house making sure all the windows were closed and locked while waiting on Will. She turned off the coffee maker and put the breakfast dishes in the dishwasher. She was at the registration desk in the foyer when the kitchen door closed.

"Finally. I thought you were doing a spa day back there in the garage."

When Will turned the corner into the foyer, Kate's heart nearly stopped.

"Wow! When did you buy a new suit?" Kate looked at Will in the mulberry three-piece suit with a white dress shirt. The tie was a perfect match of navy and wine narrow stripes. Even his shoes were glossy burgundy loafers.

"Would I make the cover of GQ?" He leaned on the newel post in a model-like pose.

"I almost didn't recognize you without your hiking boots and jeans." Kate grinned. "It's a great transformation, but I do love my engineer fiancé too."

Will chuckled. "I wish you could have seen your face when you looked up at me. I bought the suit last weekend, you know, for more formal events, like a wedding perhaps. I figured church counted."

"You look great. Now if I only had a ring for you."

He came over to her and pulled her from behind the desk. "Why don't we go to Clarksville after church? We'll get lunch and go to a jewelry store." He kissed her.

Kate thought she'd melt. He looked better than she'd ever seen him look, but he was still her Will, the same Will she'd fallen in love with so many years ago. One more weekend of guests, then the wedding weekend. *Lord, help us make it to the finish line.*

When they arrived at church, Sarah, Jane and Paul pulled in beside them. Jane popped out of the car before Paul even set the emergency brake.

"Billy! Billy!"

Will stepped out of his truck. "Good morning, Jane. How are you this morning?"

"You look so pretty!" She smiled and hugged herself.

Will laughed. "You mean handsome, don't you? Guys aren't pretty."

"Oh." Jane blushed. "I sorry. You look so handsome."

"Thank you. This is my wedding suit."

Jane looked puzzled. "Are you allowed to wear it on not the wedding?"

"Suits are more functional than a wedding dress." Will took her hand and spun her around. "And Miss

Katie didn't say I couldn't."

Jane glowered. "I don't care what Miss Katie says about it. You're MY special friend only."

Kate had exited the truck and heard all that Jane and Will had said. "Aren't we friends too?"

"No, you taking my Billy away." Her bottom lip jutted out in a pout.

Sarah hurried to Jane's side and wrapped her arm around Jane. "Now, Janie, Kate is my friend. She can be your friend too."

"No!" Jane raised her hand like she was going to strike Kate.

Will moved between Jane and Kate.

Kate cried out in recognition. "Will, look at the ring on Jane's thumb!"

The Celtic engraving around the man's white-gold ring sparkled in the morning sunshine.

Will reached out for Jane's hand. "Can I see the ring on your finger?"

She moved her hand behind her back. "No, 'cause you'll be mad. I don't want Billy mad at me."

Sarah stepped to Jane's side. "Can I see it? Show me."

"I didn't take it. Someone gave it to me." Jane took it off and handed it to Sarah. "See, it says For Will Love Forever. She said I should have it 'cause I love him forever."

Sarah sighed and turned red. "Oh, Katie! It's Will's ring, isn't it?" She handed it to Kate.

"My ring!" Jane cried out. "Don't give it to her. It's mine now. Just like Billy."

Sarah took Jane's hand. Then she handed the ring to Kate and took Jane back to the car.

Kate gasped. "Will, it is your ring. How could Jane get it?"

Will took it in his hand. "It's very nice, Katie. Thank you. I don't deserve you."

Andy walked across the lot to where Kate and Will stood. "What's happened here?"

Will put the ring in Andy's hand. "Jane was wearing this."

Andy inspected it. "How did Jane get a hold of this?"

Shrugged shoulders all around answered him.

"I don't like accusing or questioning someone with a mental disability. It's so hard to know what capacity they have to understand what was done and why it's not a good thing." Andy leaned against Will's truck. "What did she say about it?"

Kate raised her hand. "She said someone gave it to her."

"You don't have to raise your hand, Katie." Andy smiled. "Did she say who?"

"No." Kate crossed her arms over her chest. "Jane said whoever it was thought she should have it since Jane loved Will forever." Her heart hurt and whenever it did, she worried about that next unexpected heart attack.

"It's probably a long shot, but I'll take it in and have the lab swab for DNA. Anyone who has touched it may have left DNA, especially in the engraving." Andy jogged across the parking lot and snagged a plastic bag from his car. When he returned, he took out a Sharpie to write on the bag. "Who touched it here?"

"Jane, Sarah, Katie, me, and you." Will crossed his arms over his new suit.

"Cool suit! Is that what I'm buying for the wedding? Looks great." Andy wrote on the bag as he spoke. "About time I had a new suit. I'm usually in uniform or jeans." He pointed out his jeans with his polo shirt and denim jacket. "Anybody else? It's like a who's who of Robertson County. I'll take it to the lab now, so it doesn't get 'lost' before the twenty-third. I'll take possession of it as a groomsman and be sure it arrives on time."

"Thank you." Kate wandered back to the truck's passenger side.

In the background, she could hear Jane and Sarah arguing. Someone had used Jane to get to her and Will. Who? Kate didn't know many people in town. Brian was off the hook for the ring theft at least. He didn't know Jane or Sarah. They'd mentioned Viola Chastain, but Kate hadn't seen her since she was staying in the root cellar and pitched a tantrum in the backyard. Who else could it be?

Will waved to Andy and walked back to the truck; Katie was already in the cab. He guessed Katie thought it was too late to go into the service for this morning. He opened the door and stepped into the truck.

"I think my new suit requires a new truck. What do you think?"

As he expected, Katie never even heard him. How could he stop the torment of his sweet, lovely lady?

"Katie?" He touched her arm. "Are you okay?"

She looked into his eyes. "No. I'm not okay. What

should we do? Someone is trying to spook me, and they're doing an incredible job." The tears in her eyes threatened to spill over. "Should we not get married? Maybe it's just not worth the pain. I just don't know how to keep being okay with what we're experiencing."

Will's heart clenched. "What are you saying? You want to cancel our wedding?"

"I don't want to cancel our wedding, but I don't see how we move forward." Katie pulled a tissue from her purse. "Maybe we need to stay apart this week. Obviously, you need to use the garage. Let's do what we have to do. Otherwise, we need to reconsider what we're doing."

"Katie! This is the one thing I know. You and I belong together forever. Our whole lives have been about being able to be together."

"Don't you think I know that?" The tears were streaming down her face now. "I need to tell you something. When I had that heart attack in the ambulance after breaking my back, I sustained damage to my heart. I take medicine for it, Will. I can't take the stress. Do you understand? I could die from stress. Why are people trying to kill me?"

Will felt his heart breaking. How could Katie say no now? A week and a half before the wedding? After all they'd been through. He just couldn't say anything because if he did, wearing his wedding suit, he would lose it. He wasn't sure what that would look like, but it wouldn't be pretty or manly.

Will started the truck.

Katie touched his arm. "Don't you have anything to say?"

"Not now." He threw the truck in gear and drove

back to Kate's B&B. Not their house? Not their future? No! No! They couldn't let the ogres win. No way was he letting Katie go. None. He parked the truck and turned to face her.

"Listen." He took a deep breath. "No way am I giving up on us. I love you, Katie. I won't let you go. I know you love me, too. Take the week, prepare for next weekend's guests. I'll be in the garage when I'm not at the site. I am here for you always."

She sobbed. "I love you, but we don't have a place here."

"We do. It's here. Together." Will swallowed with a dry throat. "Sweetheart, please don't give up on us."

Katie took off her seatbelt and scooted over beside him. He raised his arm and wrapped it around her shoulders. "I don't want to give up. I love you."

"Rest as much as you can, my love." Will bent and kissed her, the most passionate kiss they'd ever shared. It was the kiss that would lead them to a place they shouldn't go before the honeymoon. But Katie needed to know how much he loved her and how much he was willing to do to keep her.

Chapter 25

A week without Will …

They got out of the truck. Hand in hand, they reached the porch where Will wrapped her in a huge bear hug, tears in his eyes. "Don't stop believing in us, after all these years, and all we've through. I love you, Katie-girl."

"I love you always, Will Bell." Katie hugged him back and wiped her tears from his new jacket. "You look great in this suit."

"I'll wear it on our date on December twenty-three." He struggled to keep the tears from overflowing. Someone needed to be strong.

Will let her go and watched her climb the porch steps, unlock the door, and disappear inside. He took a deep breath and walked through the backyard. As he did, Beebe came bounding from the house, jumping up on his brand-new suit. If accepting Beebe's love meant some dog hair on his clothes, he could always brush that off.

When he looked up to the house, Katie stood at the kitchen door. She raised a hand. He returned her wave, then he went on to his home away from home. Like purgatory, he wasn't home with his parents nor with Katie, just somewhere in between waiting for his new life to begin.

After changing into jeans and a t-shirt, Will sat down at the computer to check on his air transfer system. *This isn't good. It's held up by bad weather. In two weeks, the thing had to be installed and working. If not, he'd be living his own* Die Hard *movie at Christmas. At that point, the wedding is a moot point.*

The knock at the garden door startled him. He walked to the door and peeked out the window. His parents were there. How did Mom know, just know, when there was a problem? He shook his head and unlocked the bolts to let them in.

"This is a surprise visit." He smiled as best he could.

"We're taking you to lunch, Billy. We came to get you both, but Katie said you're taking a break this week. What did you do?" Mom was still in her Sunday finery, but the hands on her hips told him, this was not going to be a friendly visit. "Put on your shoes. Tell us about it while you do that."

"Yes, ma'am." He was in so much trouble. "It's not my fault, Mom. Jane showed up at church wearing my wedding ring on her thumb. All she'd say is that someone gave it to her because it's engraved For Will Love You Forever, or something like that. She said she would, so she began wearing it."

"How did she get that?" Dad sat down beside him on the sofa bed.

"Don't know. It disappeared from Katie's bedroom

during one of the intrusions. Jane wouldn't say who had given it to her." He finished tying his boots.

Mom came to him and sat on the opposite side of him. "That's hardly your fault."

"And not Katie's either. But … I didn't know that she's been struggling with a heart problem since back in the summer after the heart attack in the ambulance. The stress is getting to her."

"Is the wedding still on or not?" Dad, of course, straight to the point.

"That's hard to know. Neither of us want to cancel it." Will leaned back on the bed. "There's another fly in the ointment. I accepted a job from a biker gang that must be complete by Christmas."

"Billy! What were you thinking?" Mom always knew where to lay the blame.

"I know, I know. But the B&B isn't making money, and this contract was paying a lot for a little work, and well …"

"Biker gang." His dad, again, straight to the problem.

"Right. If the job's not done by Christmas, someone could die, me, Katie, one of you."

Mom put a hand on his knee. "Does Katie know about this?"

"Only the big picture. I didn't want to tell her anything that would get her killed, and I was told to tell no one." Will realized he'd said too much. "Oh, and the garage is probably bugged."

Dad stood. "We need to go to Shoney's. Come on, before the Church of Christ lets out in Clarksville."

Will was still in trouble, now from his parents too.

Kate watched Will and his parents walk through the back yard with Beebe bouncing all around them. His mom threw her a kiss. Maddy knew she'd be watching. Will stopped at the bottom of the steps to the kitchen. Part of her wished he'd barge into the kitchen and sweep her off her feet. But that wasn't Will. He'd respect her wishes, no matter what. And she loved him all the more for it.

Will held up the hand signal for 'I love you.' Then he continued to the front of the house to catch up with his parents.

She popped popcorn in the microwave, the last bag from the movie fest during the previous weekend. She'd need to buy more before Friday. She poured the last Coke as well. Something else for the shopping list. Popcorn and Coke. A pretty poor lunch. At Beebe's yip, she opened the kitchen door to let him in.

Kate carried her 'lunch' into the living room and camped out on the settee. She found a movie channel to stream that was showing the old Christmas movies, *Holiday Inn, White Christmas,* Alistair Sims's *Christmas Carol,* and, of course, *It's a Wonderful Life.* The day turned into night, and Kate fell asleep on the settee with Beebe on the rug at her feet.

When she woke, it was dark, and the movie playing was George C. Scott's version of *A Christmas Carol.* She stretched startling the puppy.

"Surely there's something left over in the fridge." Kate spoke to Beebe as though he would understand, and maybe he could. He stretched and headed for the kitchen. Kate followed him. After rummaging around in the fridge and freezer, she decided on a pot pie. It would take a while, but she had plenty of time. She set up the oven and prepared the pie to go into the oven.

After placing the pot pie in the oven, Kate went upstairs and changed into a nightgown and robe. With no one else in the house, it wasn't a problem to wander around in a robe as long as the doors and windows were closed and locked. The alarm was set.

The light was on in the garage. Kate plucked her phone from her pocket and opened her text function. "You don't have to sleep in the garage. You can always go to Maddy's and Porter's. It will probably be boring around here."

Will's reply was immediate. "I won't leave you alone on the property. Be sure to lock everything before you turn in. If you need me for ANYTHING, don't hesitate to call me. I'm here." He finished the message with a row of hearts.

Kate sent him an emoji throwing a kiss. She wasn't sure if she could last the week without him. Maybe that was the best reason to try to do so.

Will looked at the emoji of Katie throwing a kiss to him. He responded with the heart emoji that makes heart balloons cover the screen. Too sappy? Maybe, but he was fighting for his soulmate. The wedding was just over a week away. He wasn't sure he could cope with canceling it. Regardless, he would not leave her alone on the property. Too much had happened to believe she was safe in her own house, despite all they'd done to secure the place.

He changed into sweats. It was cold in the garage,

like always, but he could also leave his bed in a hurry without having to get dressed in an emergency. He stretched out on the sofa bed with the novel he was reading. He hadn't read very far when his phone rang. No caller ID. His heart sank.

"Hello, it's Will."

"Will Bell, it's your employer. I understand there's been a mistake made on the construction site. And that mistake caused you to be unable to do your part of the work."

Will gulped. "Yes, I sent back the part and ordered a different system. It should be in soon."

"Will the deadline still be achievable?" Demeter's end of the line made an odd clicking sound. Was the call being recorded?

"Depends on the weather and the Christmas shipment delays. I'm hopeful." Will cringed but telling him anything else would be lying. And lying to Demeter would be a fatal mistake.

"I don't feel reassured, Mr. Bell." Demeter paused. "Do you need further encouragement to achieve your part of the project?"

"I've done all I can do. Talk to your foreman about dumping that shipping container in the hole before it was ready." Will's anger rose to the surface. He'd done his due diligence.

"So, you're saying it's not your fault?"

"Yes, that's what I'm saying. I've done everything possible to get that new unit in before Christmas. Now I have to wait on it."

"I don't like waiting, Mr. Bell. I also notice that your girl is home alone tonight. Lover's spat?" Demeter's line still had an eerie clicking sound. Was it being traced? "Maybe Katie could wait for you underground without that air transfer unit. Would that speed up your installation?"

"No! Don't touch Katie. It wouldn't do any good anyway. I'm hoping to have it in a week, before the wedding." Of all the times for Katie to want to be alone!

"Well, I would hate to delay or cancel the wedding for you. I can wait until the twenty-third as long as you complete your contract before the 'I do's' take place." What was that background sound?

"Very well. Stay on it." Demeter hung up.

So much for sleep tonight.

Chapter 26

Wedding jitters …

Kate woke to a silent house. Only she and Beebe were there. She opened Beebe's crate and her own bedroom door. It shouldn't matter if her room was open if no one else was there. Beebe rushed down the stairs to the kitchen, probably to find Will.

Halfway down the stairs, she realized that the usual coffee smell was missing. She'd become spoiled with Will arriving early to start the coffee brewing. The smell of cinnamon was also missing. Most of her coffeecakes had cinnamon in them.

A truck door slammed out front. Kate ran to the front porch to see if it was Will.

She called out to him. "Will! Good morning! I'm fixing a cinnamon coffeecake. You're welcome to come share it with me."

He held up a bag from the coffee shop in town. "I'm good for now. Maybe a mid-morning snack. Oh, Katie, be sure to keep the doors locked. I love you."

"I love you." She said it but couldn't bear to shout it as he turned the corner toward the back yard. "I know, I know. It's what I asked for." She wandered back into the house and closed and double-locked the door.

She let Beebe out into the backyard and watched Beebe and Will play. After countless games of catch and chase, Will squatted down to the white lab, rubbed him, and nestled his face in Beebe's fur. He loved that dog as much as Kate did. And Beebe loved him. Finally, Will gave him one last energetic rubdown and went to his garage.

Was he safe there? Even with all the locks, Demeter and his gang could easily steal him away. What's more, Kate wouldn't even notice for a while. Had she endangered them both with this silly experiment?

Kate hurried to answer the ring on her phone. It was Maddy, not Will.

"Hello? What's up?" Kate tried to sound upbeat for her future mother-in-law.

"I think you and Will should come over. We've had a startling development on your intruder case."

"Have you spoken to Will?" Kate hated even asking if his mother knew more about his movements than she did.

"I don't know what game you two are playing, but I refuse to be in the middle anymore. He said to tell you he'd be waiting in the truck out front. See you soon."

She was ticked. Kate could tell. What's more, she couldn't blame her. Kate grabbed her coat and purse. Sure enough, Will was waiting in the truck for her.

Will got out and opened her door for her. "Good morning, again."

"Your mom's mad."

Will nodded. "Oh, yes, I recognized that as soon as I told her to call you for me. She did not take it well at all."

Kate turned and looked at his handsome face with the stylish beard stubble. "This is stupid, isn't it?"

He touched her face and lifted her chin. "No. If this is what you need to be sure, then this is what we need to do. It doesn't change how I feel. I will always love you."

Kate slid over next to him. "I miss you so much. I didn't realize that I lived and breathed with you every day."

"I know what you mean, but I don't think it's a bad thing to do this until Friday."

Will kissed her, and it made her swoon. How could she live until Friday without him?

Kate slid back over to her side of the cab and fastened her seatbelt.

Will could barely contain his desire for her. *Almighty God! Keep me in your perfect will. Contain my desire until our wedding night.* He took a deep breath and exhaled slowly. Then he started the truck.

"Are you okay?"

"No. If we weren't fastened to the seat in a truck, I'd …." He ran his hand through his hair and then smoothed it down. "Temptation is strong."

"I feel it too. I guess it's true what they say, 'Absence makes the heart grow fonder.'" She touched his hand.

Will jerked it away. "It's not my heart that's in charge just now. My heart is pure. It's my emotions that are ruling at this moment. And we're driving to my parents' house!"

Katie shrank back into the corner of the cab. "Got it."

He put the truck in drive and headed the several blocks to Chez Bell. Every moment he fought to curb his raging desire for her. It hadn't even been twenty-four hours since they agreed to limited contact. Will remembered what Joe had said about how hard it should be to live in the same house without the temptation to .... Guess Joe had been right about that. They had just managed to work together in the friend zone. Sweet Katie.

"Let's just say that I'm a man with normal desires. Don't worry. I love you, and I'll do whatever I need to do to act appropriately until the wedding night." He smiled. "You're safe with me, my dear Katie."

He pulled into the driveway at Chez Bell. "I think we're safe at my parents' house."

Katie laughed. "Unless she plans to fuss about us not talking to one another."

Will looked at her and raised his eyebrows. "Then there's that. Wonder what this is all about."

Katie shrugged. Then she pointed at Andy's patrol car in front of the house.

"Oh. It's that kind of business." Will jumped from the truck and raced around to open Katie's door for her. "I wonder what's happened now."

When she stepped from the cab, he wrapped his arms around her. "Don't forget how much I love you, no matter what may happen."

She stretched and kissed him. "Guess we better find out what's happening."

He rolled his eyes, and she giggled. "Get, you temptress."

Maddy met them at the door with her hands planted on her hips. "What kind of game are you two playing?"

Will waved a hand at her. "I'll tell you later. Why is Andy here?"

"Why am I ever where you guys are concerned? The intruder came to Chez Bell last night." He motioned to Porter who sat at the desk in the living room. He brought up the security footage on the laptop.

The time stamp was two o'clock AM. Two figures appeared at the patio door. They tried to open the sliding screen door to the family room. Will's dog Walker, an old black lab, appeared, bouncing on the glass slider inside. Lights turned on. It was clear to see who stood on the patio then.

Katie's face turned ashen. She stumbled backwards to sit on the couch. Walker snuffled at her lap. She stroked him absentmindedly.

"Right. The last people you'd suspect." Andy shook his head. "We took the two of them into custody. They're at the Sheriff's Office now. Needless to say, they are without alibi for this."

"Why were they here?" Katie hoped it was any reason except to destroy her new wedding ensemble. Anything but that.

"They planned to somehow get into the house to destroy your wedding dress." Dad spoke up. "They assumed we were country rubes without security or locks on our door. That enrages me most."

"Now, Porter." Mom patted him on the shoulder. "I just can't understand it. Hadn't she claimed to be your friend, Katie?"

"Yes. Sarah was my friend. I showed her my clothes, and then she went with me to replace the ones that were destroyed." Katie covered her face with her hands.

"She claimed to be helping her sister, Jane." Andy filled in the story. "Jane was apparently hysterical over Will marrying anyone but her, so they were somehow behind these random acts of destruction to put the wedding on hold."

Will stalked to Katie's side. "That's ridiculous. I never said I would marry Jane. She should know that." Will settled on the couch next to Katie. "I never told her I would marry her, Katie, believe me."

"But you were kind to her, and you held her hand. And you had a secret language when you parted from her. She loved you. You showed her love that no one else did. You're handsome, kind, and caring. How could she not love you? I do."

Will's heart broke at Katie's tears. "I didn't mean to make her think anything but that we were friends. How do I fix this?"

Andy spoke up. "Well, we have several resolutions. One, we can charge them with criminal mischief since they didn't actually break into the house here. They could get a suspended sentence. However, they did gain unlawful access to the B&B, potentially harming more than just Katie. The assaults on Beebe, on Katie's property, and on Katie herself are much more serious. Plus, there's the possible assaults on your guests. Not to mention the time and effort of the sheriffs, forensic lab, and TBI. Unfortunately, the betrayal of a friend is not a chargeable offense unless she used your confidence to gain access to the destroyed goods."

"I took Sarah to my room to see the first dress and pearls and shoes. I took Sarah with me to find a new dress and shoes. She knew I took them here to keep anything from happening to them."

"And there's the ring that was stolen," Will added.

"It's more than a civil case, Katie. It's a criminal case. We'll have to charge the two of them with something." Andy kneeled before her and took her hand. "I know you don't want to have them prosecuted. I'm not even sure we can prosecute Jane. Sarah is the responsible party here. She knew better and should have guided Jane to do nothing."

Katie looked up into Andy's eyes, giving Will a jolt to his heart.

"What happens now? What do I need to do?" She squeezed Will's hand.

"Come down to the Sheriff's Office so we can evaluate what the correct charges should be."

She turned to Will. "We do this together, Sweetheart. I can't do it alone."

Andy stood. "Porter, send me copies of the security footage." He pulled on his jacket. "You able to come now?"

Katie nodded. Will helped her up. "We'll be right behind you."

Chapter 27

Charging a friend …

Kate walked into the Sheriff's Office with Will holding her hand. How could she charge her friend for destroying her wedding dress? How could she not charge her? What about Jane? The whole morass made her sick to her stomach. Sarah was supposed to be her friend. I guess sisters with mental challenges come ahead of friendship. She guessed she could understand that.

"Are you okay?" Will pulled her close to his side.

"No, but what can anyone do about this?" Kate gave an involuntary shudder. She felt cold, but it wasn't the weather or the room temperature in the station. It was the idea of her friend breaking her not-so-wonderful pearl necklace, destroying her antique wedding dress, cutting up her shoes, and stealing Will's wedding ring. On top of that, after helping her choose another dress and pair of shoes, she came to Maddy's and Porter's to wreak the same damage on the new clothes.

Will pulled her close and wrapped her in his arms.

"I love you. I would marry you every day if necessary to make you my wife."

"That's not just desire, my love?"

"No, it is a covenant love borne from our friendship as children and grown into an adult kind of love shared in Christ. That's why you can trust me to always be by your side, even when we're apart."

Andy waved at them. "Have a seat there." He gestured to a row of chairs against a concrete block wall.

"Doesn't look very homey, does it?" Will helped her off with her coat.

"Homey is probably not the atmosphere the sheriff is going for."

The door to the office opened, sending with it a draft of winter. Maddy and Porter stepped in and closed the door. Once their eyes adjusted to the indoor fluorescent lighting, they spotted Kate and Will and joined them in the not-so-homey row of chairs.

"Why are you two here?" Kate took Maddy's offered hand.

"I couldn't let my daughter go through such a horrible time without her mother." Maddy pulled her into an embrace. "Your mama would never forgive me if I let you go through this alone. I'm always here for you. I don't know why Porter's here." She laughed and let go of her. "Try to relax. You are not the one at fault in this matter."

She hugged Will then sat down beside Kate.

Andy waved for Kate and Will to follow him to an interrogation viewer's booth. Through the one-way mirror, Kate saw Jane and Sarah sitting on one side of a table. Andy joined another man on the other side from them.

"I cannot believe this." Kate turned to Will's shoulder. "I don't know what to do."

Will held her. "You don't have to do anything. The case is criminal now."

"But why did Sarah do this?"

Sheriff Davis entered the viewing booth. "I've seen many things, Miss Winslow. Caring for an adult with a child's mind is hard."

Sarah's voice broke through the booth window. "I didn't steal the ring! Neither did Jane! Someone else gave Jane the ring."

"Who?" Andy's voice, though those in the booth could not see his face.

"Jane won't tell me. We also didn't leave any of those notes."

By the end of the interview, Sarah only admitted to bringing Jane to the Bell's house. Jane had claimed she only wanted to see Kate's dress. Jane had stolen the ketamine from the vet's office for someone else to use on Beebe. The pearls, the wedding dress, the ring theft, the cut-up shoes, and the brick through the window were someone else's handiwork. Kate drooped from exhaustion.

"I'm taking you home." Will took her hand and pulled her from the viewing booth.

Will and Katie returned to the house after the interrogation was over. Sarah and Jane were charged for their crimes. Katie looked as though she had been charged as well.

While Beebe jumped around them, Will carried the dog crate to the house. Katie entered the master code in the new locking mechanism and went inside with an always excited Beebe. Will took the crate up the stairs. Since the door was open to her bedroom, he took it inside. Once it was settled and restocked with Beebe's mat, towel, and toys, Beebe went in, turned around two times, and flopped inside.

Will returned to Katie. "Do you want me to look around?"

She sighed. "It should be okay. I'm going to take a nap. I'll call you if I need you."

He nodded. "Okay. I love you. Little over a week till 'I do'." He gave her a gentle kiss and went out the kitchen door to the garage.

There was only one other person who would want to wreak havoc concerning Katie. Did Viola break the pearl necklace, slice up the dress, and cut up the shoes? Did she drug Beebe and steal the ring? Was she responsible for the threatening notes? Sarah swore she'd only taken Jane to Chez Bell. Brian had just trashed the bedroom. Who had been into the house through the root cellar?

Will walked to the root cellar door and checked the lock. Sealed tight with the new combination code lock. He headed to the garage. The cold wind whipped around him as he undid the multiple locks he'd placed on the garden door.

After relocking all the mechanisms, Will flopped on the bed. He'd take a nap too except he needed to check on the shipping of the unit for Demeter. He wanted that business done.

He groaned when he checked the shipping schedule. Delayed again. At this rate, he'd be installing the unit on his wedding day. Not his first choice.

His phone rang. No caller ID. With a sinking heart, he answered it anyway. "Hello."

"We have a problem, Mr. Bell. I see the unit is delayed again." Demeter's voice raised the hair on the back of his neck.

"How can you know that?" Will suspected he'd been bugged, but hacked as well?

A dark laugh echoed in his ear. "You're a smart man, you'll figure that out."

"The geo-tag also tapped into my computer." He should have known.

That laugh again. "There's a reason I choose the smartest employees."

"If you can see the delay on my computer, you know there's nothing I can do about the situation."

He could hear the snarl in Demeter's tone. "I also know you planned a honeymoon to Scotland after the wedding next week. Don't think you can just escape the country and avoid my reach."

"What do you want me to do? I can't upgrade the shipping any more than I have." Will's heart sped up. "You need to leave Katie out of this."

"A little birdie tells me you violated our contract requirements by sharing way too much about the contract with your friend, the deputy, your parents, and most probably, your fiancée. Do you not believe me?"

Will ran his hand through his hair but didn't smooth it back. "I do, so I shared to protect myself and Katie."

That snarl again. "Hmm. What should I do about

that?"

Silence made Will wonder if he'd hung up. "Demeter?"

"I'm still here. I'm waiting for your answer."

Will took a deep breath. "Nothing. As long as I complete the work, you have no reason to do anything. I did not disclose the work site. You're safe."

A nasty-sounding laugh. "But are you, Will Bell?"

The click on the end of the call coincided with a deep shudder on Will's end.

Chapter 28

Wedding in a week …

The rest of the week had been a blur for Kate. Last-minute preparations for the final guest weekend and the wedding took a large bite of her time. The wedding cake that Sarah had been doing was still in play once she and Jane had been bonded out by Paul. It felt strange relying on someone who had broken her trust for such an important part of the wedding.

Will had been scarce. She'd seen him come and go. He'd wave on his way to the truck and call her at night to talk and wish her sweet dreams. Kate felt relieved because it seemed the break-ins had ceased.

Friday arrived quickly. Kate saw this weekend as though it was Christmas Eve. She made a Jesus' birthday cake. Stockings were hung 'by the chimney with care'. She had Christmas punch in the fridge to be warmed in a Crockpot. She made another batch of sugar cookies to be decorated or consumed plain. Christmas movies were still in the living room. Christmas music on the piano. Kate even added apple-cinnamon air fresheners throughout the house.

Kate wrapped presents for Will and his family and Sarah and Jane because she couldn't not be concerned about them. She placed the gifts under the tree.

The final touch was Aunt Katharine's Christmas dishes. Adorned with holly and mistletoe, they went with the Christmas tea set. Along with the tiered tray and teapot, the set had dinner and lunch dishes, ice cream/fruit bowls, cereal bowls, dessert plates, and candlestick holders. They'd never use it all at breakfast, but it set the atmosphere. After she placed red candles in the candle holders, everything looked ready to celebrate Christmas.

For the wedding, she'd placed poinsettias on the stairs. With the tree lights and the candles, the house looked perfect.

The first guests arrived at the stroke of three. The cuckoo announced them.

"Good afternoon. Welcome to Kate's B&B." Kate smiled and shook hands with the wife and the husband. "I'm Kate. My fiancé Will is on the premises somewhere."

"Joan and Stephen Morris."

"Here's your packet of information. The front door takes a code, so you can come and go as long as it's locked the rest of the time. You're in room five. As it turns out, there are only two couples this weekend." Kate explained the activities she'd made available.

Joan replied, "Sounds great. I think we'll freshen up and rest a bit before seeking dinner. Maybe we can go with the other couple."

"They are in room three when they arrive, so you both have as much privacy as possible. If you need anything and I'm not around, knock on room one.

That's my space."

Kate checked her watch. Three-oh-five. Will was a stickler about her being alone when guests arrived. He wanted them to see he was on the property. She shrugged. *Guess he got tied up.*

The second couple arrived about three-thirty. Will was still not with her in the foyer.

"Good afternoon! You must by Thelma and Louis Crutchfield." Kate shook hands. "Welcome to Kate's B&B. I'm Kate. My fiancé Will is normally here to greet our guests."

She got them checked in, and they also retired to their room. She overheard Thelma remark on how Christmas-y the B&B looked. Kate allowed herself some happy claps.

Where was Will? She called his phone, but it went straight to voicemail. That wasn't like him at all. Kate hurried through the house, out through the backyard to the garage. When she reached the door with the multiple locks, she realized she didn't have her keys to open them. She tapped on the door, and it swung open.

Her heart sped up as she walked into the office. His chair was overturned, and blood was on the desk. *Oh, God! Where is Will?*

Kate called Andy.

"Hey, Katie! What's happening? Been a quiet week at Winslow/Bell."

"Will's missing." Kate was determined to stay calm and not cry or become hysterical. "I came out to see why he missed the check-ins. His chair's overturned and something that looks like blood is on the desk."

Andy's voice became raspy. "When's the last time you saw him?"

"Maybe sometime Wednesday. You know, we've been taking a break before the wedding." Kate shook her head. It was foolish and left Will in danger. Someone took advantage of Will being alone.

"I'll be right there. Back out of the office and try not to touch anything."

Andy clicked off without his usual encouragement. *Guess he was scared too.* Kate went back to the house to await his arrival.

In record time, Andy screeched up into the gravel driveway. He hopped out of his patrol car, placing his hat on as he climbed the porch steps.

Kate threw the door open. Andy rushed in and took her in his arms.

"He's not getting out of this wedding that easily. I just bought that suit last night. It's a nice suit, but I probably would have bought navy if I'd had my druthers." Andy squeezed her so hard she could barely breathe.

When he finally let her go, she gasped. "I'll show you what I found."

Stephen Morris came down the steps before Kate could move. "Is everything okay? Is that the police?"

"It's a Sheriff's patrol car. Andy's a good friend. He just came by to check on something for me." Kate didn't exactly lie, but it also wasn't actually the truth either. "No worries."

He looked wary. Kate had no idea why, but she had the feeling he knew what was happening. Could he be a mole or a plant to get inside her house? "I need to join Andy in back."

She hurried back to the garden door, touching nothing.

Andy leaned over the computer still on the desk. He had on his ever-present neoprene gloves. "I think you have a message on Will's computer."

Kate walked carefully into the crime scene. "What do you mean?"

Andy waved her over. "There's a file on the computer desktop labeled 'for Katie's eyes' and the icon is three times the size of other files on the desktop. Do you want privacy to open it alone?"

"No, what I want is Will back, particularly before the wedding."

When Andy tried to open the file, it requested a password. "Any idea what the password would be? I assume it would be something you and he think about."

"Try the wedding date, 122323."

Andy shook his head.

"No, try the code for the front door master combination, 47x70."

Andy gave her a questioning look.

"How many times to forgive someone. For seven times seventy."

"Not that, try again."

"His license plate on the truck? CNS-TRCT"

"Last try, think hard."

"Or don't. Try KATIE."

"That's it!" He moved to allow her access to the desk.

She read the file aloud. "Katie, if you are seeing this file, something has happened concerning my contract. My computer has been hacked by the employer. I can't be more specific. Try not to worry about me. Let Andy track my phone."

It was all Kate could do to remain standing at the

desk. She walked over to the bed and collapsed on it. *Keep him safe, Lord. Keep him safe.*

"Katie, stay strong. I'll find him." Andy squatted beside the bed near her face. "I'll go to Chez Bell and let Maddy and Porter know what's happening."

Kate shook her head. "Every cop show I've ever watched reminds the cop not to promise things they have no control over – like life and death of a victim. Here we are. You can't promise to bring him home alive. We're supposed to be married in a week. What can I do?"

"Keep it together. Take care of your guests. It's my job to bring him home safe." Andy opened his arms, and she grabbed him and cried.

When forensics arrived, they sternly ejected them from the garage.

Kate returned to the house just as the two couples were planning to go together to eat in Springfield. She gave them some suggestions. Once they left, Kate fixed a sandwich and a Coke.

The knock on the front door startled her. She peeked out to see her future in-laws, not just Maddy and Porter but also Joe, Sally, and baby Mandy. She hurried to let them in and received and gave hugs and tearful encouragement. They also brought pizza from Angelo's.

As they ate, Porter broke the silence concerning Will's abduction. "When did this abduction happen?"

"I saw him on Wednesday evening, but with trying to get ready for guests, we didn't cross paths Thursday or today." Tears threatened to begin again. "I should have seen him those days."

Joe nearly jumped out of his chair. "So, we don't

even know when he was taken?"

Kate gave him a pleading look. "The file on his computer to me was dated today's date. It must have been sometime today."

Sally sighed. "It hasn't been that long then." She gave her husband a stern look.

Maddy had been uncharacteristically quiet. "Katie's done everything she could do for Will. She's dealt with the law officers and still has guests this weekend."

"She should send them packing." Porter crossed his arms over his chest. "She's got enough to worry about this weekend."

Maddy laid her hand on his arm. "Activity stills the mind. Having them here allows Katie time to think about something else for a few minutes here and there."

When the pizza was gone and the situation well and surely hashed, her future relatives left her to get some sleep.

Ultimately, she went to bed knowing her guests could let themselves in. She left cookies and Cokes on a tray on the registration desk.

After Kate climbed into bed, she turned her eyes to the ceiling. *Lord, I don't even know how to pray. You promise that the Holy Spirit intercedes for me. I want Will safely returned to me, so we can be united in marriage. Bar evil from having the upper hand. Help Andy discover the work site. Provide for all Will's needs. Bring him back to me. Amen.*

Chapter 29

Preparing for a wedding without a groom …

Sunday morning dawned like every other day. Kate kept a tissue in her pocket because she couldn't predict each flow of tears. She set the breakfast and rang the bell. Then she returned to the kitchen for more coffee and a bowl of cereal.

Kate heard the two couples enter the dining room. She got up and carried a pot of coffee to the dining room. "I hope you had a restful night."

Joan looked up. "You don't look like you've slept the whole time we've been here."

"Joan, that's not very kind." Her husband looked at Kate. "I apologize for her bluntness."

Kate shook her head. "No apology is necessary. She's quite right. My wedding is Saturday, and my fiancé has gone missing. I didn't disclose that because I didn't want it to impact your weekend."

Joan and Thelma gasped.

Stephan and Louis looked shocked but not quite shocked enough. They looked at each other and nodded.

Stephan spoke first. "We're with the FBI. As part

of the investigation of the bad guys at the heart of that problem, we wanted to stay with you and see what we could do from here."

Louis pulled Thelma closer. "The ladies didn't know it was anything but an unusual time to spend together. And they antique shopped while we worked with the Robertson County Sheriff."

Joan smacked Stephan's arm. "You were working this whole time?"

He fake-cringed. "I'm afraid so. That's why we spent so much time with the 'other couple'. Did you have a good time?"

Thelma nodded. "Yes, it was like Christmas Eve and vacation all at once. I'm so sorry this is happening to you, Kate. I'll pray for his safe return."

Joan came to Kate and embraced her. "I'm so sorry. What can we do to help?"

"Please eat your breakfast before it gets any colder. I'm coping. Andy's doing all he can." Kate felt the room waver like a heat shimmer in the desert. Then everything went black.

The next thing Katie heard was the beeping of a monitor. She opened her eyes to a hospital room and IVs running into her veins. She had an oxygen mask on her face. Maddy was asleep in the chair beside the bed. Joe slept on the other side of her. Joe looked a lot like Will when asleep.

She pressed the nurse button creating a loud beep. Maddy and Joe startled awake.

"How can I help you?" a disembodied voice asked.

Kate pulled the mask off. "I'm awake." Her voice was cloggy and raspy. She cleared her throat as best she could.

"Someone will be right in."

Maddy grabbed her hand. "You scared us bad, Katie-girl. I didn't want to tell Billy that you'd died on our watch while he was fighting for his own life."

Kate tried to smile, but it just wouldn't come. "Last thing I remember is discovering the guys at the B&B were FBI agents, working with Andy."

Joe stirred and leaned forward on his elbows. "Seriously, FBI agents. Guess they anticipated something like this happening."

Kate laughed. "Probably more concerned with what product the gang is bringing in at Christmas. What happened to me?"

Maddy stood and embraced her, despite the IV lines. "Not actually a heart attack, but some kind of blip. I'm sure the docs will talk to you about it."

Kate leaned back in the bed. "This does not bode well for our honeymoon. I told Will I didn't want to get married in a hospital." Tears slid down her cheeks. "Now he's missing, and I'm the one in the hospital. Now, I'd marry him wherever we're together again."

"Try to relax, Katie-girl." Maddy sat back down when the nurse entered the room.

"Ms. Winslow, you gave everyone a good scare. You got the FBI, Sheriff's, and the Bell family to the hospital." The nurse spoke while checking vitals and monitors. "So, the damage you sustained in the summer is responsible for the 'blip' you had yesterday morning."

Katie cried out, "Yesterday morning?" The monitors spiked and beeped.

"Try to calm down." She placed the oxygen mask

back on Kate's face. "You've had some messages." She brought up something on her rolling laptop. "Andy Lawrence said, 'Don't worry about Will. They're still looking for him.' Stephan Morris said, 'We're staying at your B&B, and the ladies are taking care of everything.' Louis and Thelma said, 'Get well. Everything will get better.' Any of that help?"

Kate calmed her breathing and nodded.

"That's such a pretty ring, but you should let Ms. Maddy hang on to it for you. It would be a shame to have someone steal it while you're asleep. When's the wedding?" The nurse continued assessing her while talking.

"Saturday." The monitors showed her heartbeat tick up. "But my fiancé was abducted."

The nurse finally looked at her. "That's why you had a heart episode?"

Kate exhaled. "Yes. I really can't talk about why."

A doctor walked into the room and shooed Joe and Maddy out. "Tell me what's going on to engage your heart problem."

After repeating the synopsis she'd given the nurse, the doctor ordered some relaxants to help with her regular heart medication.

"As I recall, your favorite beverages are coffee and Coke."

Kate nodded.

"Until Will is found and the wedding takes place, avoid caffeine in coffee and Coke. You have enough on your plate without adding caffeine to the mix." He added the orders to the computerized chart. "The nurse can remove all the IVs as long as you are drinking water."

"Got it. Water and no caffeine." Kate already felt the withdrawal headache pounding in her forehead. "When can I go home?"

"I'll leave orders for the headache you're experiencing. Let's check in tomorrow morning and see how you're doing then."

Will woke up with a splitting headache. His hands were bound. With effort, he was able to stand. *Where am I?* It was pitch-black except for a small lamp on a table in the middle of the space. It looked familiar. *Was it …?*

Then Will remembered. He was inside the shipping container. Closed up in the shipping container without the air transfer system. *Do not panic. Panic uses up air.* People will be working around the container during the day. They'll let in air then. As long as they find him before the wedding, he would be fine. He replayed the parts he recalled of his abduction.

Demeter was waiting for him when he entered the garage. Two of his thugs dragged him over to the desk.

"Check the whereabouts of my air transfer system, Mr. Engineer." Demeter's snarl made his skin crawl.

Will brought up the shipping information. *Delayed again.* It wouldn't come in until after Christmas according to this notice. "December 26." *It's a death sentence.*

"Which part of before Christmas did you misunderstand? If you think you are getting married Saturday, then jetting off to Scotland with your pretty lady, you haven't truly comprehended the gravity of your situation."

That's when one of the thugs bashed his head into the desk. Luckily, he'd been able to create a file for Katie to find on his laptop. He had closed the shipping notice in time, so the file was on the computer desktop. Now she just needed to find it.

The next thing he recalled was arriving at the worksite. Workmen watched as the thugs dragged him out of the van and across the ground to the hatch to the shipping container. No one did anything to help him. *So much fear.* Guess he was without enough fear to avoid this situation. *God, help me! Help Katie cope with this situation. Help Andy find me in time.*

They forced him into the hatch and down the ladder. The container had dirt filled in around it. The top was still viewable.

The thugs forced him onto the floor. His vision was blurry. Probably from having his head bashed.

Demeter looked into his face from an uncomfortable distance. His breath smelled like alcohol and weed. "Think of another way to get my air transfer system. Or suffer the consequences of this underground container without one."

After Demeter straightened up, someone hit Will's head from behind.

Once he remembered most of what had happened, he realized that the lamp on the table was actually a burning kerosene lamp, using up precious oxygen he needed to breathe. As much as he needed light, breathing was more important. He blew out the flame.

Chapter 30

Will there be a wedding?

Leaving the hospital on Wednesday was a great blessing, but Kate felt minutes ticking away on her wedding preparation time. The doctor's orders were "do nothing". How could she do nothing? When would they find Will? Her mind buzzed with a million questions that had no answers.

Maddy and Porter pulled up to the curb. The nurse helped her up into the cab of Porter's truck with Kate's new best friend, a continuous EKG, so the doctor could decide if she could go on her honeymoon! Hoping for a honeymoon was second on her list. Having Will at the wedding was her first priority. Three days. How long before they found him? Her dreams were of being in a dark container underground, gasping for breath. She feared those dreams were Will's reality.

They had shared dreams before, not like ESP or anything like that. It was more like they were on the same wavelength, sharing the same consciousness. Even though the dreams were dark, she prayed they meant Will was alive. *How long would he survive underground?*

"Ready, Katie?"

Kate tuned back into real life. "I'm sorry, I was thinking about Will."

Maddy held her hand. "We asked if you were ready to go home."

Kate nodded. "Yes, definitely." *But it's not home without Will.*

Porter and Maddy helped Kate into the house and up the stairs to her bedroom.

Joe came in with Beebe, who scrambled up the stairs and into the bed with her.

Maddy helped get the dog out of the bed into his big dog bed at the head of Kate's bed.

"Just rest, Katie-girl. I'll be downstairs fixing us lunch and dinner. Is there anything you'd like me to make?"

Kate laughed. "One of your specialties: lasagna, spaghetti, or chili."

"Now Katie, I don't put chili beans in the lasagna." Maddy laughed with Kate.

"Any of those is fine. They're the most memorable meals I've shared at your house with Will." Tears threatened again, but she was determined not to cry anymore. It didn't bring Will back nor prepare for a wedding that might not happen. Now she had to rely on God to preserve Will's life while searchers looked for him. *Lord, give them insight. It will be difficult to find an underground shipping container.*

As though someone had spoken aloud, Kate heard, "I know where he is, and I hold him in the palm of my hand."

She looked at Maddy, but she hadn't heard it or

said it.

Okay, God, it's in your hands. I trust you.

"Rest well, my dear daughter-to-be. I'll find something to fix." Maddy closed her door to the hallway.

Maddy would be the only one, besides Will, that she'd trust with the epiphany she'd experienced. For now, she needed to hold those words close to her damaged heart.

Soon, she drifted to sleep.

The darkness gave way to light when a workman descended the ladder into the container.

"Mr. Engineer. They told me you were here. I'll leave the hatch open for as long as I can."

"Can't you help me?" Will gasped for the fresh air pouring into the interior.

The man looked at him, sympathy in his eyes. "Dude, you know I can't. If I did, they'd replace you with me. I got five kids to support. Sorry." He rustled around in the toolbox at the end of the container. When he found the tool he needed, he headed up the ladder. "You're an example of what happens when you cross Demeter and his crew."

Sunlight and air continued after the man left. How long before someone decided the hatch should be closed?

A voice came to him. "I know where you are, and I hold you in the palm of my hand."

Will lowered his chin to his chest. "Lord God, I hear you and I'm waiting on you. Take care of Katie and her heart." *No doubt, Katie, we're getting married Saturday. God has this under His control.*

Footsteps sounded above him. They had not covered the container yet! A woman appeared on the ladder with a bag and a water bottle in a sling hanging over her shoulder.

"Hey there, brave man. Crossing Demeter, talking to the cops, telling people about Demeter's business. Haven't seen many people that brave. It's a shame your handsome face is going to die down here unless that part comes in before Christmas."

She set the water bottle on the table and opened the fast-food bag. A burger with fries.

"You're the waitress at the Farmacy!" Will hadn't realized how hungry he was until the smell reached his nose. His stomach clenched and mouth watered. "Thank you for bringing this down here. How am I supposed to eat it?"

"Jimmy's gonna fix you up." She gave him a half smile and climbed up the ladder.

Standing on tingling legs, Will stumbled to the table. He assumed a 'dunking for apples' stance and picked up a fry with his mouth. *Heaven!* He ate another, savoring the salty oil-cooked goodness. He needed the water, but he had no way to unscrew the cap.

"Ingenious. You really are a smart guy." One of the thugs, Jimmy?

"You Jimmy?" Will raised his eyebrows to accentuate the question.

"That dumb broad knows she's not supposed to give you any names in case that part comes in before Christmas." When he reached the table, Jimmy whipped out a switchblade.

Will flinched and moved away from him.

"Relax. I'm going to make it easier to eat." He cut the cords on Will's wrists then forced him into a folding chair. The man tied Will's legs to the chair. He dragged the table to Will. "Enjoy for now. No telling when you'll get the next meal."

Will watched as the thug climbed the rungs. *Don't close the hatch!*

The hatch slammed shut with a bang. No more air. No more light.

He felt along the edge of the table trying to remember where the bottle of water sat. When he reached it, it fell off the table. He leaned over and felt along the tiled floor. The bottle rolled away from him with his first touch. He scooted the chair a bit and tried again. Success! He grabbed the bottle, unscrewed the top, and drank the refreshing liquid.

The hatch opened again. "Sorry, dude. I forgot there's no lights yet."

Will rolled his eyes. Demeter didn't hire the brightest thugs, it seemed.

He ate the food gratefully. *Don't worry, Katie. I'm okay.*

Kate woke. She could swear she'd heard Will's voice.

Chapter 31

Strangers and hospitality …

When Kate came down to lunch, she discovered Stephan and Louis at the dining table. *The FBI guys, right. But if they're here eating at my table, they're not out looking for Will.*

"Hi." Kate stood at the end of the table. "How's the search going?"

Stephan sighed. "Too slow. I'm sure you feel it too."

Kate nodded because if she opened her mouth, she was afraid bad things might come out. Her continuous EKG beeped at her. "Sorry, I'm a little stressed." She escaped to the kitchen.

Maddy wrapped her in a big, bear hug. "Did I just hear your little friend go off?"

She nodded. "I just want them looking for Will, not laughing with each other at my dining room table." She buried her face in Maddy's shoulder. "I thought I heard Will's voice. He said, 'Don't worry, Katie. I'm okay.'"

Tears ran down Maddy's cheeks. "Praise God.

Praise God. It will be okay then. He would never lie to you."

"But how can I hear him?"

Maddy shrugged. "Weirder things have happened. I believe the Holy Spirit connects all Christians. Add to that how you and Billy have been connected for most your lives. You couldn't be closer without matrimony. God sent his message to you. Try to see it as comfort until he's back with us."

Kate nodded and began to pour a cup of coffee.

"No, ma'am. No coffee until Billy's back and the doc says so." Maddy took the cup from her and poured the liquid back into the pot. "I set up a pot of decaf for you."

Kate made a gagging motion.

"It won't be long. Take care of yourself, if not for you, for Billy. It'd be a sad thing for him to come out of his nightmare to find you too ill to go through with the wedding." Maddy poured Kate's special coffee. "Doctor how you like as long as there's no caffeine."

"Thank you." Kate dumped sugar and cream in the coffee and took a sip. Then she added more cream and carried it into the dining room to hear the status of the search. As she dropped into a chair, she saw a black shadow cross the front windows.

She nearly tipped over the 'almost coffee' and rushed for the front door. She opened it to find a large man dressed in black standing at her mailbox, rifling through her mail.

"Hey! You have no business going through my mail!"

"You must be the beloved Katie." The man laughed. "Will has good taste."

The lecherous look the man gave her caused the alarm to go off on her device.

"Oh, I'll tell Will that you're not well. Maybe that will encourage him to cooperate with Demeter. Me? I'm here to collect Demeter's air device from the mail for Will. As long as it's here by Christmas, you'll have your guy back. If not, it will be sad."

Louis and Stephan stepped onto the porch.

"Is there a problem, Kate?" Stephan stood beside her.

"This man knows where Will is and is collecting something for Demeter."

Louis whipped out his FBI badge. "I'd have to say that you're in custody then."

Stephan stepped up with handcuffs.

The man turned to Kate. "Katie really doesn't want you to do that. If I don't return to the work site shortly, Will might find his situation much more difficult."

Kate stepped back a step. The alarm went off at a higher pitch.

Maddy joined the party on the porch. "Whatever you are doing, I must insist you stop. Katie cannot take this stress in addition to Billy's absence."

"I think we can talk to you at the Sheriff's office before getting you back to your gangster master." Stephan clicked the handcuffs into place.

Kate sat down on the porch swing and wrapped her arms around herself. The December wind whistled through the porch, rattling the windows. She closed her eyes and thought as hard and loud as she could. *Will, I need you back. I love you. Do anything you can to stay alive and to come home. I got your message. Get mine.*

Stephan dragged the man from the porch to a

waiting government vehicle.

Louis kneeled before her. "We'll take care of this situation. Trust us to anticipate the danger as well as the resolution of Will's abduction. Your job is to be ready to marry your man on Saturday."

Kate nodded.

Maddy pulled her to her feet and brought her into the house. She sat her down in her favorite chair in the sitting room and wrapped a knitted blanket around her shoulders. Then she brought her coffee and sugar cookies. "The lasagna can be ready soon. Then I think rest is in order, sweet girl." She kissed Kate on the forehead. "I'm sorry this is so hard. I love my son, but I know God's hand is on him. God loves my son more than I can even imagine. You just need to take care of you right now. That and prayer, those are our jobs."

Kate shuddered and snuggled into the warmth of the blanket. Sleep took over her stress.

The dark was suddenly illuminated. Blinded by the light, Will saw a worker climbing down the ladder. The lights they'd installed yesterday worked well, but nobody had left any of them on for Will. Sleeping in a chair with his legs zip-tied to its legs was uncomfortable in many ways.

The worker dragged the card table over to Will and set out an egg sandwich with hash browns. Coffee in a takeout cup would have to do. Will couldn't even remember what day it was.

"Dude, you better hope that part comes in today or

you're gonna miss that wedding."

"It's Friday?" Will blinked. Time had run together despite his attempts to keep track. The workers came and went at odd intervals. And his head pounded from the probable concussion. "You know, I have no control over Christmas shipping times, especially tied up underground."

The man shrugged. "Demeter gets what Demeter wants. Someone will come in to help with your other necessary functions." He nodded over to the bucket in the corner and shuddered. "Good luck." The man climbed the ladder to the real world.

Will drank the tepid coffee and took a bite of the sandwich. He'd had a wonderful dream. Katie came to him. Her voice echoed in his head.

Will, I need you back. I love you, Do anything you can to stay alive and to come home. I got your message. Get mine.

He wasn't sure how he heard her or what she meant about getting his message. Her voice helped him stay sane though regardless of the source. He praised God for any comfort He would give to him.

In addition to the head injuries, Demeter's thugs had beaten him at least once a day. His ribs hurt among other physical damage. Could he even stand at the bottom of the stairs and walk with Katie into the living room tomorrow? Once he'd finished his food, his eyes refused to remain open. His head found rest on the table until the next worker came down to pity his situation.

Will jerked awake at the sound of the hatch closing. He heard a ruckus on the topside of the container. It sounded like the earth mover started up.

Were they burying the container? Hope fluttered and attempted to leave him. *There's a hatch. Katie's not giving up on me. I'm not alone.*

Dirt caved into the top, creating echoes of the shifting metal container. Will took a deep breath and prayed.

Keep me safe and sane, God. Help Andy find me.

Another load of dirt hit the top. The lights flickered and went off. Darkness heightened Will's stress level. Demeter's workers were not the brightest bulbs in the pack. They must have clipped the electric line.

I still have air. I've eaten. People know I'm here if they have the gumption to speak to the police.

Suddenly the heavy equipment stopped.

What was happening? Were they fixing the electric line?

The hatch opened. A flashlight beamed into the darkness and into Will's face.

"Will! Thank God we found you! Katie will be elated." Andy's voice,

Will covered his eyes from the flashlight. "Is that you, Andy?"

"It is. We're getting out of here. Stephan and Louis have Demeter and his thugs in custody. TBI has rounded up the workers and are hauling them to Nashville to determine their amount of culpability in this operation." Andy clipped the zip-ties on Will's legs. "Can you stand? How do you feel?"

"Besides a bashed-in head and probable broken ribs, I'm great." He attempted to stand, but his knees gave way.

Andy grabbed Will's arm and put it over his shoulders. "I got you, friend. Let's just get you up the ladder."

Will climbed the ladder, shaking at each rung. Finally, he could see the sky and an ambulance standing by.

"Will!" Katie's voice.

Hands helped him out of the hatch onto solid ground, then he collapsed. Snow swirled around. Soon arms wrapped around him.

"It's me, Will, it's me." It was Katie's voice, but sunlight made it hard for Will to see her. "Maddy's here too."

"I love you, Katie. Is it still Friday?"

"Yes, my love. It's Friday."

Paramedics squeezed into the space. "Excuse me, ma'am, we need to assess his injuries and get him to the hospital."

Her arms released him into the care of the emergency health workers.

Chapter 32

Can there be a wedding?

Kate paced back and forth outside Will's hospital room waiting for the opportunity to sit by his bed, whether he was awake or asleep. The EKG continued to beep.

"Kate Winslow! What are you doing?" The man in the white lab coat took her arm and led her to a bench. "I didn't give you a portable EKG to have you attempt to score the highest number of alarms!"

Kate shook her head. "I can't help but have alarms. My fiancé is in that room after spending three days underground. Our wedding is tomorrow." The alarm sounded again.

"I understand, but if you have a heart attack, you'll be in a hospital room instead of on a honeymoon. Do you understand the cost?"

"Yes, sir."

"Here's what I want you to do. Go home and go to bed. Rest. If there's a wedding tomorrow, you need to be rested." Dr. Randall put his hand on her shoulder. "If I can get you into Will's room, can you go home for tonight?"

"Okay, I'll do that." Kate didn't want to leave Will, but she also wanted to be able to marry him if he was okay to do it.

Dr. Randall slipped into Will's room. A few minutes later he stepped into the hall and beckoned Kate into the room. She hurried to see Will.

Will saw her and grinned. "I must be hallucinating. The most beautiful woman in the world just wandered into my room."

He was bruised and battered. The monitor connected to him beeped. But he was still her Will.

"Oh, Will, are you going to be okay?"

She took his hand. He kissed it.

"By tomorrow, you mean." Will frowned. "I don't know, my love. Depends on if they let me out of here in time."

Kate kissed his hand. "I understand. I just promised my doctor I'll go home and go to bed myself. I'm ready whenever you are."

Will nodded. "Have I told you I love you?"

"You have. I love you too."

"Go home, Katie. Take care of you. I'll come home as soon as they let me."

Kate nodded. She held back her tears and kissed him. "Later, my love."

Maddy drove her back home. She turned off the security alarm and stepped into the dark, silent house. After all the activity for so long, the house seemed dead. The mistletoe, once so happy and celebratory, seemed dark, dead, and overdone. Without Will, the house had no life.

Kate entered the kitchen and flipped on the lights. On the table stood their three-tier wedding cake. Sarah had dropped it off in the middle of Will being rescued. Who had let her in? She dragged a finger through the perfect icing and licked it off. Wonderful, just like everything else Sarah did. Would Sarah ever speak to her again? She snapped a picture with her phone.

The beckoning fridge mocked her. She opened it to get a Coke. Then she put it back. No caffeine. Kate closed the fridge and flipped off the lights and headed upstairs to bed after arming the security system.

Her lace wedding dress hung on the closet door. Her sparkling sandals were on the shelf. Maybe someday. Beebe was delighted to see her. Kate let him out, and they snuggled.

As Kate crawled into bed, she heard a sound in the walls. Kate grabbed her phone and called Andy. "It's Kate. Someone is in the inner hallways. Can you come?"

"I'll be right there. Find a hiding place."

Kate pulled Beebe out of the crate, and they hid in the closet. She heard the wall open into her bedroom. Steps headed toward her dress. Who could it be? Whoever it was could enter the house through the root cellar. Could it be …?

The lights flipped on.

"Stay where you are!" Andy's voice.

A rush of people entered the room. A struggle ensued.

"You are under arrest. You have the right to remain silent …"

The closet door opened.

"Come on out, Katie. We have your intruder."

Andy reached out and took Kate's hand. Beebe jumped out of the closet, snarling and growling.

"You have to protect me from that animal!"

Kate came out and realized that the woman handcuffed in her bedroom was Viola Chastain. "What are you doing here?"

Beside Viola was a can of red paint, the same color as the church vandalism. "I had to stop you from marrying Will. You know I love him. You should have never moved to Adams. Will would have married me."

"You've been the one coming in through the root cellar. I should have known after you lived in the root cellar last summer." Kate's hands flew to her face. "The cake!"

Viola began hysterical laughter. "I had Jane convince Sarah that it would be so much better to deliver it early. She's so easily manipulated."

Kate flew down the stairs to the kitchen. In the light of the moon, she could see the destruction. She hated to even flip on the light.

Andy entered behind her and turned it on for her. "Oh, Katie."

She turned to his chest and wept.

He comforted her the best way he could. "Will's been found and is recuperating at the hospital. The culprits are all discovered. We kept her from destroying another dress."

The beeper on the EKG went off.

"Are you okay, Katie?" Andy wrapped her in a hug. "I know Will is your soulmate, but I'll always love you too."

Kate took a deep breath. "I need to go to bed. Do whatever it is you need to do, Andy."

By then, she could hear Viola laughing in the foyer.

Andy led Kate from the kitchen and turned out the light. "I'll get the forensic team out here tomorrow. Get some rest." Andy shook his head. "Come on, Viola. We'll give you a free ride to the station."

Will lay in his hospital bed listening to the hospital night sounds: beepers going off, the rush of nurse's shoes on the tile floor, the moaning and crying of other patients. It wasn't his first choice to be here, stuck in a hospital bed by IVs and monitors. But he also knew he needed to be here with his concussion, dehydration, various open wounds, and shock.

He needed to sleep, but he couldn't turn off his brain. Katie said she didn't want a hospital wedding, but here they were. It looked like their best option. Someone had recovered his phone from Demeter. He turned it on, but it had practically no power. Time enough for one text message?

"Katie, we can get married anywhere tomorrow. If I can't come home, come here in your white dress. No matter what, we should make this happen. We've waited way too long. I love you."

He hit send as the phone shut down. *Did it send?* He pressed the call button to the nurse's station.

The disembodied voice funneled into the room. "How can I help, Mr. Bell?"

"Any chance you have a phone cord I could borrow?"

Chapter 33

Do you take this man?

Kate saw the text from Will after she woke with sunshine in her face. After she read it, she looked out the window. A fresh dusting of snow covered everything. A good day to start a fresh life with Will. Will was safe, and the culprits had all been captured. The intruders in the house had been identified and arrested. Andy was in charge of Will's ring. No cake, what did it really matter?

In the end, all that mattered was the two of them. They'd already pledged their love and lives to each other. The wedding was the final piece to start their lives together.

After a shower, she threw on leggings and a Belmont sweatshirt and headed downstairs for awful coffee and destroyed cake. In the light of day, the destroyed cake looked even worse. However, the bottom tier looked salvageable.

Maddy found her there, with a soup tureen full of broken white cake. With delicate strokes, Kate removed everything from the top of the bottom tier. Then she placed the cake topper on the bottom tier.

"What do you think?"

"What happened to your cake? Sarah brought it by yesterday." Maddy took Kate's phone and saw the picture of it before and after Viola's cake destruction. "Oh, Katie. It looks great. If we slice it thinly it should be fine."

"I was thinking about all this wedding cake." She showed the tureen to Maddy. "What if we used it to make cake pops?"

Maddy grinned. "Make lemonade."

"What?"

"When life hands you lemons, make lemonade." Maddy hugged Kate. "When life gives you two tiers of crumbled wedding cake, make cake pops. What do we need?"

Kate found a recipe online. "Lollipop sticks, white melting candy wafers, sprinkles of some kind, and a piece of Styrofoam to stick them in." Kate grinned. She could salvage the cake! "Have you heard from Will this morning?"

Maddy wrote down the list of necessary ingredients. "Porter went to the hospital this morning, hoping he can come home this morning or afternoon. I haven't heard anything. You?"

Kate began stirring the cake and icing together. "He sent a text last night after I finally got to bed. He suggested having the wedding at the hospital if he was not able to leave yet."

"But neither one of you want that." Maddy pulled Kate into a mother bear hug.

"No, but we do want to get married, today if at all possible." Kate hugged her back. "I wonder if Sarah has any icing left." She picked up her phone and found Sarah's number.

"Sarah, it's Kate."

"I can see that on my phone. How are you doing?" Sarah sounded tentative. "How do you like the way the cake turned out?"

Kate couldn't think of any way to sugar-coat the situation. "Well, it was beautiful before Viola Chastain showed up."

"Oh, no! How can I help?"

"I was able to save the bottom layer and the cake topper. The rest I scraped into a soup tureen. We're going to make cake pops, but I think I need more icing."

"I have all the ingredients you'll need. I'll be right over."

"Thank you. That will save Maddy a trip to the store."

Sarah went quiet. "It's the least I can do for my friend. I owe you so much more after all you've been through, particularly my part in it. I'll be right there."

Maddy leaned against the counter. "What did she say?"

"She'll be right over with all the stuff we need for cake pops." Kate slipped into a chair. "More important, she called me her friend. I was afraid after the ring incident with Jane and the attempted break-in that we couldn't repair our friendship."

Both of their phones rang.

Kate moved to the dining room. "Will! What do you know?"

"They're letting me go this afternoon after I've been here twenty-four hours. I heard about Viola. I'm so sorry." Will sounded distant.

"Not your fault. Sarah's coming over, and we're making cake pops with the destroyed cake."

"Andy didn't tell me about a destroyed cake. How will it be with Sarah after what's happened?"

"The bottom tier survived Viola's fury." Kate tried to present the news with as much positive spin as she could. "I don't know about Sarah. I guess we'll see when she gets here. If not, I guess I'll not have a matron of honor."

"What's a cake pop?"

Kate rushed through a brief description. "You take cake and crumble it. Next you mix in frosting. Then you form small balls of cake and icing, put a stick in it, and coat it with candy melts and sprinkles."

"Ingenious."

"You sound weary. Rest. I'll see you soon. One way or the other. I love you."

"Back at you, my love."

Kate sighed. She wanted him home, but she also wanted him well.

At the beep of the security chime, Kate hurried to greet Sarah in the foyer. "Come in."

Sarah burst into tears. "I'm so ashamed of my role in your wedding disruptions. Jane was inconsolable, and I wanted to help her. Viola took advantage of her. I have no excuse for being at Maddy's and Porter's with Jane. If you don't want me to be your matron of honor, I totally understand."

Kate took Sarah into her arms. "I forgive you. Our code for the front door is based on an important scripture. In Matthew 18:21-22, Peter asks Jesus, 'Lord, how many times shall I forgive my brother or sister who sins against me? Up to seven times?' Jesus tells him, '… not seven times, but seventy-seven times.' In other versions, he says seven times seventy. The point is I am required to forgive. I want to forgive you."

"You still want me in the wedding?"

"Yes. And I still want to be your friend. Will you be my friend?"

Sarah hugged Kate. "I would really like that."

"Let's salvage my wedding cake then."

Days in the hospital felt like weeks to Will. Dad had been there with him until it was time to open the hardware store at nine. Saturdays were his 'bread and butter,' he always said.

After lunch, he watched the clock on the wall opposite his bed tick off the minutes while he waited to be released. Would he even be able to greet his bride at the bottom of the staircase? Could he even stand long enough to say, "I do"?

Will pulled out the drawer in the bedside tray table to reveal the mirror inside. He looked as bad as he felt. He shoved it back under the tray. A shower would help him get the dried blood and dirt out of his hair. It would also chew up some of the waiting time and tell him if he could stand for the time it took to shower. His beard needed trimming back to that 'fashionable stubble' Katie liked too.

After a shower and a shave, Will put on the clothes Dad had brought: some sweats from his room at Chez Bell. They were a skinny teenager's clothes. He hadn't worn them for years, but it was better than a hospital gown or the clothes he'd been abducted in.

He sat in the chair beside the bed after getting dressed. He must have fallen asleep in the chair because the doctor startled him awake. The clock read three-thirty.

"I hear you're anxious to get married this evening. What time is the wedding?"

"Seven." Will felt disoriented and more than a little dizzy as he pushed up from the chair.

"Whoa, what's happening?" The doctor's eyebrows met in the center of his forehead. "Do you feel dizzy? Nauseated? Out of control?"

Will shrugged. Answering yes to any of those questions would mean another night in the hospital.

"Look I get that you need to marry your girl, but couldn't you wait another day or two?" Call her up and let's conference call it."

Will called her.

"Are you on your way? These cake pops are so cute. It looks like we meant to destroy part of the cake for this purpose. Sarah brought extra buttercream frosting and repaired the bottom tier. It looks like it was meant to be only one tier."

"Katie. You're on speaker with the doctor and Joe, who just walked in." The silence on the line Will felt in his soul. He understood the heartbreak of waiting one, two, three more days.

"What's going on? Do you need to stay in the hospital?"

Dr. Aiden nodded to Will. "Hey, Kate, this is Dr. Aiden. Will's been up and took a shower and dressed. He took a little nap, but he's dizzy. This indicates that the concussion is still compromising his stability. I'd like to watch him for another day or so. I understand that would postpone the wedding. Consider rescheduling it to Christmas Day or the day after."

"Of course. Whatever helps Will come back to me whole is what we should do. Okay, Will?"

"I don't like it, Katie."

"We can't have you passing out during the wedding or spending our wedding night in a hospital. Most of our guests know what's going on anyway. It wouldn't take long to let people know." Then she went silent again.

Will interrupted the silence. "Are you doing all right?"

"My doc says I'm on the road to having the most cardiac events in twenty-four hours. And I'm not allowed to have coffee or Coke."

Joe laughed. "Isn't that what Katie subsists on?

Katie answered. "And destroyed wedding cake today."

"Ooh, I'm coming over for that." Joe rolled his eyes. "Cake is the best part of a wedding."

Will threw a straw at him. "Hardly the reason to get married."

Dr. Aiden cleared his throat. "Kate, are you okay with postponing the wedding so Will can heal?"

"Of course. Whatever he needs. I'll talk to Will later. Thank you. Joe, you're always welcome." Kate hung up.

Dr. Aiden pointed to the bed and helped Will move there.

He laid his aching head on the pillow.

Joe held out his hand. "Give me your keys to the

garage, so I can bring you properly fitted clothing. These need to be donated to a middle school."

Chapter 34

Christmas promises …

Christmas Eve. They were to have been married by now and on their way to Scotland for their honeymoon. Kate picked up the tickets to Scotland and called the airline. She wasn't sure when they could go. Will might be released today, so he wouldn't miss Christmas, but who could know?

"British Airways. How can I help you today?" The voice was cheerful enough.

Kate feared a big hassle to change their reservations. "I need to change our honeymoon travel dates on our airline reservations."

"Can you give me your reservation identification number?"

Kate gave the agent all the pertinent information.

"When would you like to fly, Ms. Winslow?

"Could we fly on December 26 or 27?"

After much ado, the flights were changed to accommodate their wedding plans.

Kate sighed and laid her head on the table. How long would it be until Will was out of the hospital?

The cuckoo sounded nine o'clock. The front door opened accompanied by the security chime. Kate stood up and walked to the foyer to see who was there. When she saw his dark hair and crutches, she knew it was Will. Her slow gait changed to a run.

"Will!"

He leaned against the front door and dropped his crutches, so he could hold her up in his arms.

"I'm home!" He grinned and kissed her.

"And I am so glad to see you. After my doctor ruled I couldn't see you as long as he was monitoring my heart, I missed you so much." Kate nuzzled into his neck against his beard. "I just changed our airline tickets to Scotland."

Will held her close. "Great! I was worrying about them, but I didn't want you to worry. When can we go?"

"December twenty-six is the new flight. The twenty-seventh and beyond is booked solid."

"Then I suppose the wedding must take place today or tomorrow. Christmas Eve or Christmas Day?"

Kate puzzled over the choice. "Today. And we'll have Christmas day to spend with your family. It's Baby Mandy's first Christmas after all."

"True. Could we sit down somewhere comfy?"

"Of course." She led him into the sitting room and helped him get settled in the matching chair to her favorite one. Once he was as comfortable as he could be, Kate settled next to him. "How did you get home?"

"Joe drove me. Mom and Dad were at church. What do we need to do to have a wedding today?" He winced in pain.

Kate winced with him. "Are you sure you're able

to do this? We could postpone it a week or so to give you time to heal. I can change the tickets again.”

Will looked her in the eye. His love for her was evident. “We’ve been waiting all our lives. I refuse to let Demeter make us wait any longer.”

Kate nearly swooned. “We need the minister. We have the punch ingredients and the cake and cake pops. Your family. That’s all we have to have.”

“What time? I suspect I’ll need to rest a lot today.” He winked at her. “You know, an early bedtime wouldn’t hurt me.”

“You’ll probably need to sleep.”

He shook his head. “You’re probably right.”

Kate stood and helped Will out of the soft chair. Then they walked back through the garden to the garage. She unlocked all the deadbolts for him and opened the door. The blood was still on the desk. She grabbed a paper towel and dampened it then wiped up the majority of it.

“Don’t worry about it now. We have other things to be concerned about.” Will took off his jacket and hung it up on its peg. Then he carefully lowered himself to the bed and propped the crutches next to the bed. “I’ll be okay. Go ahead and get the ball rolling for an intimate wedding in our own house.”

She sat beside him. “I’m so glad you’re okay. I was so worried.” She kissed him.

He nodded. “Darling, I was determined not to miss us.” He kissed her back.

Kate stood. “I’ll let you rest. Call me if you need something. Lunch, company, coffee, et cetera.”

“Et cetera is later tonight.” Will made his eyebrows dance.

She laughed and went back to the house.

Six-thirty on Christmas Eve. Kate was dressed in her gown, hoping Will was actually up to this formality. They were partners in every way except marriage and its benefits. In reality, there was no reason to do this right now, but Will was insistent that it be today.

A soft knock on the door interrupted her thoughts. "Come in."

"It's Sarah." She poked her head in the room. "Is it okay to come in?"

Kate waved her in. "How is everything downstairs?"

"The cake is out of the fridge and should be fit to eat by 7:30 or so. The punch is iced, mixed, and ready to serve. The cake pops are getting rave reviews for beauty. Hope they taste as good as they look." Sarah wore the dress she bought at the last bridal shop they'd visited. It had a white velvet bodice, a red sash, and a red/green/black plaid velvet maxi skirt.

"I love the dress on you. Very Christmasy."

Sarah curtseyed and plopped on the bedside. "You look beautiful. Will is a lucky man."

"No, I'm the lucky one." Kate dabbed at her eyes, trying to keep her eye makeup from running. "How is Will?"

"He's rough. I don't think he's going to last very long tonight. You're right to worry. He proclaims his intention to go on with the festivities anyway." Sarah embraced Kate. "Try to accept whatever comes tonight. He loves you and wants to claim you as his own forever on Christmas Eve."

Another knock on the door startled Kate. "It's

Maddy. Okay if I come in and check on you?"

Sarah opened the door. Maddy wore a sparkly green pantsuit with silky wide legs. A red rose corsage adorned the top.

"I have something for you." She squatted down in front of her and presented a beautiful box.

Katie took the box, bewildered by the gift. When she opened it, a two-strand pearl necklace was inside. "My pearls? But it was only one strand before."

"Porter and I decided you needed an upgrade and had our friend include the second strand." Maddy hugged her.

"Thank you so much. I'm overwhelmed."

Sarah helped her with the clasp. "They're perfect."

"Are you ready, Katie? You look beautiful. Billy can't wait to see you. I wish your mama was here to see this day. She and I used to muse about my Billy and her Katie getting married, making us sisters of some kind. I miss her today."

"Me, too." Kate sobbed. "I'm so glad I have a place in your family."

"Always and forever, sweet Katie." Maddy hugged her and kissed her cheek. Then she took a tissue and wiped the lipstick off. "Be careful walking down those stairs."

"Yes, ma'am." Kate smiled at her.

"I think I hear our entrance music. I'd better go let Joe seat me in front."

Trans-Siberian Orchestra's "Christmas Canon" played from the iPod. Kate stayed out of sight while watching Maddy and Porter walk into the living room. She hadn't wanted Porter to fall down the stairs while escorting her. Nor did she want the poinsettias falling off the stairs. Kate would descend the stairs alone.

Sarah handed Kate her bouquet of white roses and Stephanotis. Red and green velvet ribbon wound within the bouquet and cascaded down the front of Kate's dress.

"You're beautiful." Sarah choked up.

"I'm glad you're still my friend after all this mayhem." Kate hugged her. "Be careful on the steps."

Sarah headed down the stairs to the "Christmas Canon."

When she reached the bottom, Will moved into position at the bottom of the stairs in his mulberry suit. He had discarded his crutches and held onto the newel post. Kate might be holding him up tonight. The music changed to the traditional wedding march.

Will looked up the stairs into Kate's eyes. Kate gasped. He smiled and beckoned her to him. She grinned back at him, held the banister with one hand and the bouquet and her skirt with the other. She took the first step toward him and their forever after. Each step brought her closer. Everyone else disappeared until Will was the only person she saw. The bandages and bruises were inconsequential. His smile grew larger, and his eyes sparkled. Those same eyes had greeted her on every adventure when they were children. The same eyes held her future adventures and his love for her.

When she reached him, he took her in his arms. He whispered in her ear, "I love you. Be mine for the rest of our lives."

She nodded and whispered in his ear, "I love you forever."

He gave her his elbow. They walked to the front of the living room filled with the people who mattered in their lives to pledge their love to one another.

Try this new Christmas book!
Christmas Market Romance

Chapter 1

Christmas chore …

The world milled around Amalia in Charlotte-Mecklenburg Airport. Blasting public address announcements assaulted her body, her inner introvert ready to cower in a corner. This trip got harder every year. She was getting older and more alone than ever. Going to Germany to live with her family and run their Christmas kiosk for the Christmas season would not make it any better.

"Announcing a gate change for Flight 351 from B3 to B23. That's Flight 351 to Cologne-Bonn, Germany, will now leave from B23."

Amalia groaned. It was hard enough getting a month's worth of clothing and Christmas packages to the airport. Now she had to lug the carry-on farther down the concourse. And it wasn't easy with a cane. She should have brought the rollator walker, but she didn't want her family to know just how handicapped she'd become since last Christmas. She'd make it work.

While she was looking at the wall monitor to determine the correct gate, a man came out of nowhere and barreled into her. Amalia fell over her carry-on and landed on the carpeted concrete walkway.

"Oh! I am so sorry." The man reached for her hand, the one with the cane. "Oh, did I hurt you? Can I help you get to your gate?"

Amalia jerked away from him and made a quick assessment of her body. She waved away his hand and made the elaborate effort to rise from the floor without help. "I'm fine. I don't need any help, even if I did." She blinked, then reached for her carry-on bag.

"I'm Justus Sullivan. Let me get that for you." He grabbed the rolling bag. "Would it help to hold my arm? What gate are you heading to?"

"I'm going to B23. A gate change for my flight. I can get there just fine by myself, Mr. Sullivan." Amalia tried to wrest the roller bag from his hand.

"What does it hurt to accept some help?" Justus took her hand and placed it in the crook of his elbow. "Come on. I'm headed to B23 and Cologne myself. What's your name?"

Not wanting to make more of a scene than they'd already created, Amalia resigned herself to accepting his help as far as the gate. That would be the last she'd see of him. "Amalia is my name."

When they reached the gate, Justus made sure she was seated in the priority boarding area. "Can I get you a coffee, tea, soda? I'm getting something already. It's no problem."

Amalia had hoped to get coffee, but pulling a bag and handling a cane gave her no hands to carry coffee.

And she couldn't leave her bag at the gate to go get it. "Sure. A café mocha would be great." She opened her crossbody travel purse to get a $5 bill out.

"No, I'll get it for you. It's the least I can do." He shrugged her off and headed to the coffee bar adjacent to the gate.

An older woman sitting nearby leaned over toward Amalia. "Such a sweet man. Your husband?"

Amalia laughed. "Heavens, no!"

"Maybe if you play your cards right?"

"He just bowled me over in the middle of the concourse, so he helped me to the gate." Amalia waved away her comments.

The lady leaned closer. "I don't believe in coincidences. I believe God orchestrates our connections with others. He's quite handsome, endearing, and kind. Those are good qualities in a husband. Just saying." She nodded and went back to the book she was reading.

Justus arrived with coffee not long after. "Mocha for the lady." He handed her the hot cup. "Be careful."

"Thank you, but you didn't need to buy me coffee." Amalia felt her face growing hot.

"I'm traveling on business. I try to take advantage of the opportunity to see people and not just rush from one place to another. Clearly, I was not doing either when I ran into you." Justus sipped his coffee. "If you want, I can leave you alone."

Amalia struggled with the choice. Was it a coincidence that they'd met? Did God orchestrate this meeting with this handsome man? Was he her future husband?

She cleared her throat. "You can stay here if you'd

like. Why are you headed to Cologne?"

"Like I said, business. I'm a lawyer, and we're orchestrating a merger with a business in Cologne to expand our market into Europe. It's a little hilarious. My company sells perfume."

Orchestrating? That word again. Amalia laughed. "I find it unlikely that 1709 Eau de Cologne would be willing to share the market."

Justus shrugged. "Maybe, maybe not. Is that the fragrance you're wearing?"

She nodded and took another sip of coffee. "My brother buys me a small bottle for Christmas every year. It's a thing."

"Is your family in Cologne then? Is that why you're going?" He leaned closer toward her as the airport PA started again.

"Yes is the simplest answer." Amalia had no desire to explain further, no matter how handsome he may be. Coffee did not buy him the rights to her family situation.

Justus knew a shutdown when he heard it. Clearly Amalia didn't want to share. He finished his coffee and got up to throw the cup away. He wandered over to the gate agent who was stacking paper and stapling.

"How's our flight going? On time?" He smiled at the harried agent.

"Not sure. The plane isn't here yet. But they still have time. Do you have a connecting flight in Cologne?"

"No, Cologne is my destination. I just wondered if I should buy food while I wait."

The man chuckled. "My answer to that is always buy food if you get the chance. It probably will taste better than what you'll be served on board."

Justus laughed outright. "Sounds like good advice. The young woman in priority boarding is disabled and stubborn. Can you watch out for her while I buy food?"

"She's nice to look at. Sure, I'll keep an eye out. The stubborn ones are always worth the extra effort." The agent grinned. "If you know what I mean."

He knew what the agent meant, but he wasn't trying to conquer or win her. Justus just wanted to make sure she arrived in Cologne safely into her family's arms.

Justus sat beside her. "The agent says the plane may be late and getting food is always a good idea over airplane food. Is there something I could pick up for you at the food court?"

"You don't have to get me anything." She looked offended.

"I know I don't have to, but I'm going for something. I'm willing to pick up something for you too." He tried a friendly smile. "What do you want?"

Amalia thought for a moment. "Perhaps fried rice and orange chicken from that Chinese food place, but you must let me pay for my food."

"It's a deal." He waited while she dug in her purse. "Do you want something else to drink?"

She looked up at him as though she was seeing him for the first time. "No, I still have coffee." She handed him a $20 bill and smiled. "Leave your backpack with me. I can keep it safe. It's not like I'm going anywhere else ... quickly."

Justus chuckled and dropped the backpack with his laptop in the seat beside her. "I'll be right back, Amalia."

When Justus returned with the Chinese food, people were streaming from the gate door. Apparently, their plane had landed. He dodged the jet-lagged zombies filing into the airport, finally fording the river of humanity while carrying the bag of Chinese food. He arrived at priority boarding to find Amalia frantically scanning the area.

"I'm back. I see the plane has arrived." Justus gave her a wink.

She gave him a wry smile. "I was afraid you were delayed. Thank you. I can eat it on the plane if I can carry it somehow."

"How about I roll your carry-on and wear my backpack while you carry the food bag and maneuver your cane? Where is your seat?"

Amalia groaned. "Economy class. On the aisle so I can get in and out easier."

"Wouldn't business class be easier on you?" The words were barely out of his mouth when he knew he'd made a gaffe.

She twisted her mouth. "I would love to ride in the front of the plane with the wealthy and fortunate ones. Sadly, a cripple doesn't make as much money working for a charity foundation. My family doesn't have the money to fly me to Germany. So economy is my only choice. I assume you are one of the fortunate few then?"

"I'm an idiot. Please forgive me. My law firm is

paying for my ticket in business class." He debated what to do to not seem like such an idiot. "Listen, let me go check with the gate agent. If there's room, let's upgrade you to business class, so we can continue getting to know one another."

Justus jumped up before she could protest. When he reached the gate, the agent laughed at him.

"You two are entertaining. A silent movie of grand gestures and protests. How did you say you met?"

Justus exhaled slowly. "Could you see if any seats are available in business class near me for the lady? I have reward points to upgrade her seat."

"Ooh, another grand gesture." The agent whose nametag read 'Bob' checked the screen. "Actually, the seat beside yours is unclaimed. What's the young lady's name?"

"Amalia. I don't know her last name yet. Like I told you, she is stubborn."

The man chuckled as he looked for her in the database. "Ah, Amalia Edgar." He named the cost for the upgrade and applied Justus's reward points to the cost. "Good luck to you, Mr. Sullivan." The machine spit out a new boarding pass for her.

"Thank you. I think it will be helpful to her and hopefully for me as well." Justus turned and looked toward her. "Ooh, she looks mad." He hoped he hadn't stepped over the line too far.

Simple Cake Pops

https://www.allrecipes.com/recipe/244964/simpl e-cake-pops/

Cake pops are perfect for birthdays, baby showers, weddings, or any special occasion where sweet treats are needed! This recipe is simple to make with any flavor cake mix or frosting.

Submitted by **Miss Amy**

Tested by **Allrecipes Test Kitchen**

Prep Time:30 mins
Cook Time:30 mins
Additional Time:1 hr 30 mins
Total Time: 2 hrs 30 mins
Servings: 18
Yield:18 cake pops

Ingredients

- 1 (15.25 ounce) package yellow cake mix (such as Betty Crocker)
- 1 cup water
- 3 large eggs
- ½ cup vegetable oil
- 1 (16 ounce) container prepared chocolate frosting
- 18 lollipop sticks
- 1 (14 ounce) bag chocolate candy melts
- 1 (.75 ounce) tube decorating icing
- 1 tablespoon multicolored candy sprinkles, or as needed (Optional)

Directions

1.   Preheat the oven to 350 degrees F (175 degrees C). Grease a 9x13-inch baking dish.

2.   Beat cake mix, water, oil, and eggs in a bowl using an electric mixer on low speed for 30 seconds. Increase speed to medium and beat for 2 minutes more.

3.   Pour batter into the prepared baking dish.

4.   Bake in the preheated oven until a toothpick inserted in the center comes out clean, 28 to 33 minutes. Remove from the oven and cool completely, at least 1 hour.

5.   Crumble cooled cake into a large bowl.

6.   Stir frosting into the crumbled cake until mixture is sticky and starts to come together but is not too smooth. Refrigerate until chilled, for at least 30 minutes.

7.   Roll cake mixture into eighteen 1 1/2-inch balls and place on a baking sheet.

8.   Place about 1/4 cup candy melts in a microwave-safe bowl. Microwave on high until melted, about 20 seconds.

9.   Push a lollipop stick halfway into each ball of cake mixture.

10.   Gently dip balls into the melted chocolate to coat, then place upright in a block of Styrofoam.

11.   Decorate with candy sprinkles while chocolate coating is wet. Repeat to make remaining cake pops, melting more candy melts as needed.

12.   Enjoy!

Recipe Tips

You can use any flavor or brand of frosting or boxed cake mix for these cake pops. If you use a different cake mix, just follow the instructions and ingredient amounts on your package to bake the cake. Ingredients 1 through 4 (above) pertain to the Betty Crocker mix used in this recipe.

After Step 4, you can freeze the cake for up to 2 weeks. When ready to make the cake pops, just thaw the cake fully (3 hours at room temperature or 8 hours in the refrigerator) and continue with Step 5.

About the Author

<u>www.dianeetatumwriter.com</u>
<u>tatumlight@gmail.com</u>

Diane E. Tatum began writing in grade school with short mystery stories, a play performed by her sixth-grade class, and a dictionary of supernatural beings. High school found her writing serial fiction with her friends, including developing characters and plot lines through hand-written notes.

Her first book, *Gold Earrings,* is an outgrowth of a high school creative writing class. Her historical Christian series is called *Colonial Dream.* This book is number nineteen. Her other novels are listed below.

Diane has also taken on the role of freelance editor

for her publisher Winged Publications.

In addition to her writing career, Diane taught middle school language arts for 11 years. She also has served as an adjunct professor of English at Motlow State Community College.

She is loved and supported by her husband, Ken, and their two sons and daughters-in-law. Their four young grandsons are a joy to them both. Diane and Ken have a rescued racing greyhound named Iggy and a Jack Russell puppy named Trevor; both add excitement to their home in Tullahoma, Tennessee.

Gold Earrings
Mission Mesquite
Oxford Fairy Tale
Colonial Dream, Book 1: A Time to Fight
Colonial Dream, Book 2: A Time to Love
Colonial Dream, Book 3: A Time to Choose
Main Street Mysteries #1: Kudzu Sculptures
Main Street Mysteries #2: The Gemini Conspiracy
Main Street Mysteries #3: Attic Visitations
Main Street Mysteries #4: DNA Secrets
Mainstreet Mysteries #5: Disappearing Diaspora
MISStletoe Romances: Dreaming of a Wedded Christmas
Nevermind Time: Cecilia's Y2 Key
Unordinary Romance: Finding Love in the Fog of Aphasia
Summer Secrets: Hiding in the Highlands
Mysteries at Kate's B&B, Book 1: Surviving Renovation
Mysteries at Kate's B&B, Book 2: Trauma at the Fall Festival
Mysteries at Kate's B&B, Book 3: The

<u>*Thanksgiving Murder Mystery Dinner*</u>
    Mysteries at Kate's B&B, Book 4: Christmas Wedding Disruptions
    Coming soon!
    Christmas Market Romance
    Lonely Christmas Honeymoon on the Rhine
    Colonial Dream, Book 4: A Time to Create

For more info about the Bell Witch:

The story of the Bell Witch is taught as part of Tennessee History in 7th grade. John Bell's death is the only investigated and authenticated death caused by an evil spirit in the U.S.

Bell, Charles Bailey, A Descendant. *The Bell Witch of Tennessee* (the black book). 1934.

Ingram, M. V. *Authenticated History of The Bell Witch and Other Stories of the World's Greatest Unexplained Phenomenon* (the red book), including "Our Family's Trouble" by Drewry Bell. 1894.

"The Bell Witch Cave." *Ghost Adventures* Season 13 Episode 5, (This seems to change seasons and episodes).

Websites:

https://bellwitchfallfestival.com/

www.bellwitchcave.com/

https://adamstennessee.net/community/businesses/